Hugh McCal

Land law (Ireland)

fourth report from the Select Committee on the House of Lords together with the

proceedings of the Committee, minutes of evidence and appendix

Hugh McCal

Land law (Ireland)
*fourth report from the Select Committee on the House of Lords together with the
proceedings of the Committee, minutes of evidence and appendix*

ISBN/EAN: 9783742805522

Manufactured in Europe, USA, Canada, Australia, Japa

Cover: Foto ©Andreas Hilbeck / pixelio.de

Manufactured and distributed by brebook publishing software
(www.brebook.com)

Hugh McCal

Land law (Ireland)

Note.—The Evidence of Witnesses whose names are in *Italics*, is to be found in the Minutes annexed to the Third and to the present Report.

FOURTH REPORT.

BY THE SELECT COMMITTEE appointed to continue the inquiry, commenced by the Select Committee of last Session, into the Working of recent Legislation in reference to LAND in IRELAND and its Effect upon the Condition of the Country; and to whom leave was given to Report from time to time.

ORDERED TO REPORT,

THAT the Committee have met and considered the subject-matter referred to them, and have examined several Witnesses in relation thereto.

1. Your Committee made their First Report on the 28th of April 1882. In it they made certain recommendations with regard to the procedure of the Commissioners and Sub-Commissioners under the Land Act of 1881, and also certain proposals for facilitating the purchase by tenants of their holdings under that Act.

2. Your Committee made a Second Report on the 1st of August 1882, in which, after stating that they had not then completed the inquiry into the matters referred to them, they reported the additional evidence taken by them up to that time, and recommended the re-appointment of the Committee in the next Session.

3. The Committee was accordingly re-appointed on the 9th of March, 1883, to continue the inquiry commenced in the Session of 1882.

4. The Committee at the commencement of the present Session examined several additional witnesses, some of whom were officially connected with the working of the Land Act, and the evidence of these witnesses appeared to the Committee to be so important that they thought it right by a Third Report to report the Minutes of the Evidence to the House, in order that, if it was desired to produce evidence in contradiction or explanation, opportunity might be given for doing so. No evidence, however, of this kind has been offered, and the Committee, having examined some additional witnesses, have **now** to make their final Report.

5. The Land Act of 1881 dealt mainly with three subjects; first, the settlement of judicial rents; second, the purchase by tenants of their holdings; and third, emigration. All the other provisions of the Act may be considered as auxiliary to these, its main features. Of these, the first, namely, the settlement of judicial rents, was by many of those responsible for the measure considered to be a problem of a temporary and exceptional character, in order to secure, as it was hoped, a moderate amount for tenants dissatisfied with the conditions of their tenancy until the time arrived when they could be converted into owners or provided for by means of emigration. *Three objects of Land Act. 1st. Judicial rents. 2nd. Purchase. 3rd. Emigration.*

6. The Committee, in inquiring into the working of the Land Act, have found that with regard to emigration the Act has not been worked at all. The Emigration Clauses have entirely failed to answer the purpose for which they were intended. The evidence, however, taken by the Committee shows conclusively that with regard to some parts of Ireland it is by emigration only that the *Emigration clauses have not been worked.*

[130.] a 3

the suffering and discontent which have prevailed in those parts can be overcome, and that in those parts of the country it is not a question what amount of rent should be assigned to the holdings of the tenants, inasmuch as, even if they paid no rent whatever, they could not live on their holdings (Bird, 1744; Thompson, 8184; Tuke, 7507, 8, and *passim*; *Robinson*, 1459).

7. With regard to the purchase by tenants of their holdings, your Committee in their First Report stated that, for the reasons therein mentioned, the arrangements made by the Act to promote such purchases must be taken to have failed. Your Committee do not think that there is any amount of business proved to have been done since their First Report was made which should lead them materially to qualify this statement (Appendix C.), and having in their First Report fully expressed their opinion upon this subject, they do not think it necessary now to dwell further upon it. They only desire to say that they have been misunderstood in being supposed to have recommended an unlimited or extensive expenditure of money or guarantee by the State at any one time. Your Committee expressly stated that it was "for Parliament to decide the extent to which the operation of purchase should at any one time be carried, and the amount of the funds which should from time to time be allocated for the purpose," just as it is for Parliament to define the extent to which the operations of purchase under the present Act shall at any time be carried.

8. Your Committee will now advert to the working of the Act with reference to the settlement of judicial rents.

9. Some inconveniences of a minor character have been pointed out to the Committee in the procedure of the Commissioners for settling judicial rents. It is stated that much time and expense would be saved, and the attendance of the Bar facilitated if the Commissioners, in hearing contentious cases argued by counsel, would hold their sittings in Dublin at the Four Courts, in which counsel are generally engaged, and not in their house in Upper Merrion-street, which is a mile and a half distant from the Four Courts (*Kabane*, 9—16). The limit of 10l. valuation, below which a landlord has not a right to demand from a tenant the particulars of improvements intended to be relied on by the tenant, is much complained of (*Smith*, 345—357), and there appear to be sufficient reason for withdrawing this limit, especially if the application to the Court to order particulars, or fuller particulars, were, in all cases, allowed to be made, as it is contended it should be, to the Court of the Sub-Commissioners in the country, and not to that of the Commissioners in Dublin (*Smith*, 354—9). The changes made from time to time in the constitution of the Sub-Commissions are much deprecated, as they remove from a particular locality persons who have become acquainted with the circumstances and the character of the land in that locality, and whose determinations have become precedents for settlements out of court in the neighbourhood between landlord and tenant (*Baldwin*, 1149—1156). The Committee will afterwards notice the reasons which would appear to have led to some of these changes. It is also desired, and your Committee think with good reason, that the Sub-Commissioners should sit in a greater number of places, and in fact wherever there is a petty sessions court, and thus save a great loss of money and time at present incurred (*Baldwin*, 1166—1170). Complaint is also made of the want of regularity of some of the courts in country places in observing the hours appointed for their sittings (*Chamber*, 1666—1676).

10. The Committee cannot but look with great regret upon the manner adopted in settling judicial rents under the Act. This duty, the most important, and at the same time the most difficult, to be discharged under the Act, was, in the first instance, assigned by Parliament to the three Commissioners named by the Act, whose names and standing were stated to be a sufficient guarantee that the duty would be effectively and impartially discharged. The Commissioners, however, proceeded to delegate the whole of this duty to the Sub-Commissioners appointed under the Act, who now number 83; and they made this delegation without having themselves heard any of the cases in the first instance, in the course of which hearing they might have enunciated some general principles to be followed, or established some precedents to serve as examples, and without having laid down any code of instructions or any general principles according to which the Sub-Commissioners should act. Some at least of the Sub-Commissioners were desirous of receiving such instructions, and one of them, Professor Baldwin, states that he thought at the time "it was a frightful thing to let them

" loose

"house on the property of landlords and tenants without any instructions." Specific questions were put to the Commissioners as to the manner in which the Sub-Commissioners should act, but were not answered (*Reeves*, 180, 312—314; Litton, 3311—3344, 3426—3436; *Baldwin*, 1012—1019, 1029—1036, and 1073).

11. The result has been that which under the circumstances might naturally have been expected. The various Sub-Commissions throughout the country laid down no principles upon which they proposed to act; they have not, in their judgments, explained the grounds on which they acted; there has been an absence of anything approaching to uniformity between the decisions of the different Sub-Commissions (The *O'Conor Don*, 2100, 2101), and the decisions of the same Sub-Commission have frequently been inconsistent with each other (*Smith*, 427); no statement has been made as to the method by which the judicial rent has been arrived at, and no explanation has been given of the manner in which improvements made by the tenant have been dealt with or estimated, as affecting what otherwise would be the fair value of the land (*Atkinson*, 4499—4504; *Holmes*, 92, 114, 117—131; *Reeves*, 207—210; *Foley*, 700, 701, 712—718, 741—742, 801—803, 812—813; *Smith*, 412—414; *Wright*, 1585—1588, 1594—1600; The *O'Conor Don*, 2099, 2100, 2101). It has been impossible to ascertain in what manner the Sub-Commissioners, in holdings subject to the custom of Ulster, have treated improvements; whether they held the tenant-right to include all improvements, or whether they estimated their value separately (*Smith*, 376—381). The same Sub-Commission, differently constituted, in regard to its members, has reduced two sets of farms, adjacent and similarly circumstanced and rented, the one by 16 per cent., and the other by 30 per cent. (*Groar*, 7272—7276).

12. By this want of uniformity in the decisions, and the impossibility of ascertaining any principle upon which the valuation has proceeded, there has been interposed the most serious difficulty in the way of making, out of court, those amicable arrangements which it is so much for the benefit of the landlord and tenant to encourage, while, on the other hand, it is the opinion of those well acquainted with the feeling of the tenants, that the wide difference in the decisions will engender a fresh crop of discontent among those who consider that terms less favourable have been awarded to them than to their neighbours (*Litton*, 12—14; *Smith*, 427—431, 617 and 618; *Chambre*, 1794; *Baldwin*, 1032—1033, 1157—1160; The *O'Conor Don*, 2100, 3101).

13. The Committee have endeavoured to ascertain from the Commissioners and from such Sub-Commissioners and persons conversant with the proceedings in the Land Courts as they have examined, whether any insight could be obtained into the principles upon which the valuation of land in Ireland under the Land Act has been and is now proceeding, but they have not succeeded in doing so, and it does not appear that those who preside in the Courts of the Sub-Commissioners have been able to form any conception of the nature of these principles, if they exist.

14. It would appear that the reductions have sometimes been the greatest where the improvements of the tenants were the least (23rd, 1679 *King-Harman*, 7364—7366). The improvements, indeed, seem to have been dealt with in the most haphazard and irregular manner, and the evidence received with regard to their existence, state of repair, and value, to have been of the most unsatisfactory description (*Gray*, 1074—1078, 1982, 1983, 2001—2003, 2040—2043).

15. Little or no difference appears to have been made whether the rent was an old rent, and regularly paid for a number of years, or whether it was a modern rent (Bird, 4043; *Peasey*, 3492; *Kennedy*, 6681; *Holmes*, 141; *Foley*, 702—704; *Wright*, 1601—1619). "The Sub-Commissioners," says one of the witnesses, "seem to be under the impression that their mission is to reduce rent. I think the principle is to give a reduction varying from 25 to 40 per cent." (*Johnston*, 6472). One of the official valuers himself states, in his evidence, "In every case that goes into Court, whether right or wrong, the tenant "gets more or less, from what I have seen. (Q.) He always gets a reduction, "or almost always?—Almost always, except that there might be one case out "of 20 or 10 on a property in which he would not get a reduction" (*Gray*, 1900—1901). See also The *O'Conor Don*, 2101). The same official valuer, who was

was employed by several Sub-Commissions, states that he was in the habit of deducting an arbitrary sum of about 15 per cent. from the letting value to represent the tenant's right of occupation (Gray, 1070—1072). In other words, the occupation having been obtained by the tenant upon a contract to pay a certain sum as rent, his occupation was then treated as an asset of his own, to be set against and applied in reduction of the rent which he had agreed to pay.

Deterioration, how treated.

16. There appears to be strong ground for believing that in many cases where the land has been deteriorated by the act of the tenant, he has had the benefit of his own wrong, and the land has been valued in the condition in which it stood, and not according to what would have been its value if properly cultivated (Dunwoody, 5878—3860; Guthrie, 6764—6767; Wright, 1581, 1682—1688, 1684).

Arithmetical process of reduction.

17. Your Committee have had laid before them a considerable amount of evidence from which they think there is much reason to conclude that in some of the Sub-Commissions, where reductions have been largest, a simple arithmetical process has been adopted by reducing the rents, by adding two, three, or four varying estimates of the value together, and dividing by the number of such estimates. Examples of this will be found in the Evidence and Appendices (Smith, 954—957, 419—421, 442—445, 448—455, 1836—1841; Robson, 1180—1186, 1848—1851, and 1358; Gray, 1672—1676). This proceeding, if it has really been followed, involves a grave dereliction of duty on the part of the Sub-Commissioners, and is unjust both to landlord and tenant.

Landlords with high rents fare the best.

18. The judicial settlement of rents under the Land Act was recommended to Parliament mainly to meet the cases, said to be comparatively rare and exceptional, in which land was over-rented or rack-rented in Ireland; but it would seem that in the arbitrary process of reduction which has been adopted, a landlord who has unduly raised the rent of his land, fares the best, for the reductions do not, as a rule, appear to be usually greater on estates highly rented than on estates low rented (Atkinson, 4613; Bird, 4634; Delmore, 4212; Thompson, 5962—5963; Johnston, 6474—6474). Reductions varying from 22 per cent. to 38 per cent. and upwards have been made on several of the oldest and best managed family estates in Ireland (Digges, 5289; Dunwoody, 5986; O'Callaghan, 6867; King-Harman, 7361; Foley, 821—822; Baldwin, 1600—1570).

Legal Sub-Commissioner takes no part in valuing.

19. The dangers incident to the appointment of a number of Sub-Commissioners, with jurisdiction practically amounting to a power of transferring property from one person to another, were supposed to be counterbalanced by the circumstance that each Sub-Commission would have, as its President, a skilled and experienced lawyer, whose learning and professional reputation and standing would be a guarantee that the vast powers of a Sub-Commission in settling rents would be exercised in an impartial and judicial spirit. Few or no questions of law are now, owing to the mode of procedure of the Sub-Commissioners, raised before them, and their great and continuous work is that of settling judicial rents. In this work the legal Sub-Commissioner appears to take no part. The legal Sub-Commissioner is, in the language of Professor Baldwin, reduced, so far, to the position of a cypher. He takes no part himself in the valuation of the land, he is ignorant of the principles upon which it is valued by his colleagues, and he has no means of knowing in what way they apply the law to the facts of the case, or whether they apply it correctly (Baldwin, 1148, 1303, &c.; see also Atkinson, 4528; Moran, 144—151, 231, 237, 240, 241; Reade, 451). It would appear doubtful whether the Commissioners are aware that this is the position of the legal Sub-Commissioners, for Mr. Justice O'Hagan states that "all the Sub-Commissioners are Judges, and all of them noted, hear the evidence and decide upon it" (4777); whereas Mr. Litton, in answer to the question (3401), "Then I suppose the legal Sub-Commissioner does not attempt to form an opinion upon the land," replies, "Not upon the question of the value of the land," and in answer to the question (3401), "So that it is entirely handed over to the two Lay Commissioners?" replies, "It is, upon that technical point"; but inasmuch as Mr. Foley, one of the legal Sub-Commissioners, states (375—377, 591—593) that he was told by Mr. Forster, when Chief Secretary to the Lord Lieutenant, on his appointment as legal Sub-Commissioner, that he would not be expected to value the land, it must be taken that the latter is the correct view of the legal Sub-Commissioners' duty.

20. Much

30. Much dissatisfaction appears to be felt as to the manner in which these valuations take place. The rapidity with which the valuation is made is stated to be incompatible with any adequate examination of the land (Prey, 1910—1949; Smith, 2088). The lands have frequently been visited at a time when, by reason of weather or floods, no proper inspection could be made (Biel, 4691, 2; Saukey, 6886—6947). Formal evidence is given in Court, but much is, or may be, afterwards said upon the ground in the way of statement and assertion, unaccompanied by any of the checks under which evidence is given (Bird, 4788—4799). This is the more open to objection because no map or plan is produced, giving a proper delineation and measurement of the farm to serve as a guide for the Valuers, or Sub-Commissioners, when they go upon the land, and without which map or plan no valuation can be safely or effectually made (Baldwin, 1060—1124; Grey, 1967, 1968, 2040, 1).

No proper record of improvements allowed for.

31. Complaint is also made that there is no sufficient record showing what improvements have been proved to have been made by the tenant, and have been allowed for in affecting the rent. The Committee in their first Report expressed an opinion that some record should be made of such tenant's improvements as were proved in evidence; and they stated that they had heard with satisfaction that the Commissioners had, since the commencement of the inquiry, adopted a rule for the purpose of meeting this complaint, and that the Sub-Commissioners would, henceforward, be required to specify the improvements made by the tenant. The Committee regret to find from the evidence of Mr. Baldwin (1064—1069) that the form adopted by the Commissioners in order to meet this complaint has proved useless; and they must express again their strong opinion that the respective interests of landlord and tenant cannot be properly dealt with, and the settlement of judicial rents cannot be placed upon a satisfactory basis, unless there is made, and preserved, a distinct specification of the improvements established by the evidence, and of the value assigned to them in the settlement of rent.

The principle of Mr. Baldwin approved but absent in practice.

32. The Committee must also repeat what was, in substance, stated by them in their first Report, that next to the publicity of the proceedings in Courts of Justice, they consider the greatest security for justice being done lies in the rule being adhered to, that the judges should state the reasons for his decision. They concur in the statement of one of the witnesses before them (Bird, 4697), "I see no reason why a Court of this sort should not follow the example of "every other Court. There seems to be no reason why it should not state the "gross yearly value of the land, whether the land has been deteriorated, and "whether they have allowed for that, or whether it has been improved, and "how much they have allowed for that. Then the landlord can see where that "tip is circumscribed with the gross amount of rent, or that he is satisfied with it, "but that he thinks the reduction for improvements too great, or the allowance "for deterioration too small."

Sub-Commissioners why removed.

33. There is little doubt that a strong impression prevails in the country, that where Sub-Commissioners have not reduced rents to the point to which they have been reduced by other Sub-Commissioners, and have thereby become unpopular in a particular district, they have been removed to other districts, and that these changes have led to greater reductions (Johnston, 6479; Smith, 616, 9; Holmes, 96—99; Chambres, 1787, 8, 9; Grey, 1866—1867, 1968—82). The mere existence of such a feeling is, in the highest degree, unfortunate, and it is much to be regretted that anything should have been done to give rise to it.

Right of appeal; is it effective.

34. The Land Act gave to any person aggrieved by any order of a Sub-Commission, a right to have his case reviewed by the Head Commissioners. This right of appeal would be materially enhanced by affording to all parties the opportunity of obtaining from a superior court a fresh and unprejudiced hearing of any case in which the inferior court was supposed to have miscarried. The Committee will proceed to consider whether, in the working of the Act with regard to appeals, this expectation has been answered.

Procedure of Commissioners a review of that of Sub-Commissioners.

35. The Commissioners do not themselves visit or value any farm. They are provided with official valuers, one of whom inspects the farm which is the subject of appeal, and makes a report upon its value to the Commissioners. The Commissioners have this report before them, and, where the rehearing is conducted in regular course, they proceed with this report before them, to review the evidence in Court tendered by either side, and when the evidence is closed

closed, the report is communicated to the parties; but the parties are not allowed to cross-examine the valuer upon it, or to re-open the evidence. The procedure of the Commissioners may therefore be described as exactly the converse of that of the Sub-Commissioners. The Sub-Commissioners, in the first instance, prefer to hear in Court all the evidence which is adduced, and then the two non-legal Sub-Commissioners, having heard the evidence, go upon the land and apply to that which they see upon the land the evidence which they have already taken and sifted, and thus form their opinion as to the value. The Commissioners, on the other hand, send, in the first instance, a valuer on to the holding, who, without hearing any legal evidence, places a value upon it, and reports it to the Commissioners; and any evidence which the Commissioners may hear is heard after, and not before, the valuation thus arrived at. It is not surprising that, in this state of things, one of the Sub-Commissioners should state it as his opinion that, if the mode of procedure of the Commissioners be right, the proceedings of the Sub-Commissioners are wrong; while, if the system of the Sub-Commissioners be right, the procedure of the Commissioners must be wrong (Baldwin, 1239).

26. The official valuer, when he goes upon the land, necessarily finds himself in want of information with regard to the boundaries, the circumstances of the farm, the improvements that have been made, and the time when, and persons by whom, they have been made. The valuation at which he arrives must be more or less dependent on those and similar considerations, but, upon all such matters his information must be derived from statements made to him on the land, often upon hearsay, and always without the security or check of oath, or cross-examination. And it must be often impossible for the Commissioners to discriminate between his conclusions, arrived at from ocular inspection, and those arrived at from statements made to him (Smith, 676—683; Baldwin, 1222—1228).

27. Although the Commissioners withhold from the parties the report of the valuers until the conclusion of the case, they have latterly furnished them at the commencement of the hearing with the figures showing the amount of the valuation put upon the farm by the valuer. It is stated, and the result of a number of cases tends to confirm the statement, that where the official valuer's report agrees with the judicial rent fixed by the Sub-Commissioners, it is referred to as a ground for confirming the decision, but that where it fixes a valuation in excess of the Sub-Commissioners it is disregarded (Holmes, 79, 80; Smith, 605, 6). It is further stated that, with comparatively rare exceptions, the decisions of the Sub-Commissioners are affirmed, and that any real hearing on appeal seldom takes place, inasmuch as the Commissioners put it to the counsel for the appellant whether they can hope to disturb a decision of the Sub-Commissioners where it tallies with the report of the valuer, and, the appellant, after such an expression of opinion, feels it useless to proceed (Holmes, 39, 45, 115—116; Petry, 820, 821; Wright, 1559—1564; Baldwin, 1230; Smith, 409—411, 427—435, 568—570, 591—597, 608—610, 619, 633, 1654).

28. The Commissioners have not, either in affirming, or in the few cases in which they have varied the decisions below, laid down or given any explanation as to any principle on which judicial rents were to be ascertained (Holmes, 47, 53—58). If they had done so they might have avoided the suggestions which has been made that in some cases the arithmetical process of adding together different estimates of rental and dividing them has been adopted by the Court of Appeal (Baldwin, 1352—1357, 1359—1362; Wright, 1582, 1583, 1617 and 1618).

29. The Committee cannot avoid arriving at the conclusion, from the statements of the witnesses already referred to, and from other evidence (Baldwin, 1816—1822), that the proceedings of the Commissioners have not tended to create confidence in them as an appellate tribunal, and the combined operation of the functions of the Sub-Commissioners and Commissioners appears to be such that, whereas it was supposed that a tribunal was created for the purpose of dealing judicially with exceptional cases of excessive rent, there has been set in motion a process of valuation of rent for the whole of Ireland, and of compulsory letting at that valuation, in which the work of valuation is done by two Sub-Commissioners, without any professional or technical qualification, without any principle, standard, or rule for their guidance, with no obligation

to explain the grounds of their decisions, and with an appeal that is little better than illusory (Smith, 521), 3; Baldwin, 1016, 7; 1161—1165; The O'Conor Don, 2060).

30. The evidence produced before the Committee has not gone to shew that there is any strong probability that the reduced rents fixed by the Commission will in any time of difficulty or agitation be better paid than those to which the lands were previously subject (King-Harman, 7487; Foley, 659). It is further pointed out, that the remedy for recovering rent is seriously affected by the Act of 1881, inasmuch as where the rent is under 100 l. a year—that is to say, in the case of the vast majority of the tenants in Ireland—ejectment for the non-payment of rent must at the peril of being deprived of costs, be brought in the County Court, the sessions of which occur only four times in the year (Hussey, 5572—5560).

31. The Committee find that just in proportion as the Act of 1881 has destroyed competition as an element entering into the adjustment of rent, it has given to competition a greater force and prominence in raising the price obtained on sales of the tenant-right or tenant's interest in the farms (Atkinson, 4551; Brown, 130—163; Foley, 345, 730—734; Chambre, 1818, 1819). They have appended to their Report a table of the prices recently given in sales of farms in different parts of Ireland (Gray, 1052—1054). It is difficult to resist the conclusion that if by the Act of 1881 tenants have—on principles sound or unsound—been protected as regards the annual sums agreed to be paid by them in order to obtain their holdings, they suffer now still more as regards the gross sums they have to pay on obtaining a holding in the only way in which they can now obtain it, namely, by purchase.

32. While for the interest of the tenants in their farms there is a free market and a high price, it is clear upon the evidence that land in Ireland is, in the case of owners, practically unsaleable (Fitzmaurice, 4790; Wright, 6269; Sankey, 6566, 7; O'Callaghan, 3891; Greer, 7315; Foley, 655; and other witnesses). No money can be obtained on mortgage even where the security is ample, and the capital will come into the country. Landlords, where they continue to reside in the country, are largely reducing their expenditure, and many of those hitherto resident are ceasing to reside (Bigoe, 5414—5419; Hussey, 5661—5666). The relations formerly subsisting between the landlords and tenants have been dislocated or destroyed; a large portion of the produce of the country is being expended in law (Thompson, 5273; Hussey, 6549; Fitzmaurice, 5786, 5; Johnson, 6454); an alteration for the worse has occurred in the habits and industry of the tenants (Lloyd, 7154; King-Harman, 7476, 7); they have become demoralised, and they readily lend themselves to the hope of fresh agitation and a new Land Act (Dobevoody, 5056—5060; Baldwin, 1235).

33. It is unnecessary to say that proceedings which have resulted in a compulsory reduction of rent for a long and extendible term of years—a reduction with an average approaching 20 per cent., and rising in many cases to 30 per cent. and upwards—must produce serious loss and injury to owners of every class; but the Committee have had laid before them a mass of evidence, which apparently does not admit of contradiction, shewing the disastrous effect of these proceedings upon those owners of land whose property is subject to incumbrances and charges, frequently placed upon it and by themselves, and whose means of living were derived from the free margin of income after paying the interest on those incumbrances and charges, and the expenses of management of the property. The effect of the recent legislation has been, as to many such owners, to sweep away the whole of the margin upon which they depended for their subsistence, and to reduce them in many cases to poverty or ruin (Bird, 4643—4651; Hayes, 3350—3350; Hussey, 3560; Fitzmaurice, 3790—3791; Wright, 6257—6262; Sankey, 6304; 6545; Johnston, 6462—6466; Kennedy, 6575—6580; Hamilton, 6086—6091; Gubbins, 6601—6606; Barton, 7043—7057; Lloyd, 7140; Greer, 7292—7298; King-Harman, 7980—7980; Baldwin, 1240—1253).

34. And the Committee have directed the Minutes of Evidence, together with an Appendix, to be laid before your Lordships.

6th July 1884.

ORDER OF REFERENCE

Die Martis, 6° Martii, 1883.

LAND LAW (IRELAND).

Moved, That a Select Committee be appointed to continue the inquiry, commenced by the Select Committee of last Session, into the working of recent legislation in reference to land in Ireland, and its effect upon the condition of the country (The Viscount Hutchinson): *agreed to.*

Die Veneris, 9° Martii, 1883.

Select Committee on: The Lords following were named of the Committee:

Duke of Norfolk.	Earl Stanhope.
Duke of Somerset.	Earl Cairns.
Duke of Marlborough.	Viscount Hutchinson.
Duke of Sutherland.	Lord Tyrone.
Marquess of Salisbury.	Lord Carysfort.
Marquess of Abercorn.	Lord Kenry.
Earl of Pembroke and Mont-	Lord Penzance.
gomery.	Lord Brabourne.

The Committee to appoint their own Chairman.

LORDS PRESENT, AND MINUTES OF PROCEEDINGS AT EACH SITTING OF THE COMMITTEE.

Die Lunæ 28. Maii 1883.

LORDS PRESENT:

Marquess of Salisbury.
Earl Stanhope.
Earl Cairns.

Lord Tyrone.
Lord Carysfort.

The EARL CAIRNS in the Chair.

Order of adjournment read.

The Proceedings of the Committee of Tuesday, the 8th instant, are read.

The course of proceeding is considered.

Ordered, That the Committee be adjourned till Friday next, at Twelve o'clock.

Die Veneris, 1° Junii 1883.

LORDS PRESENT:

Marquess of Salisbury.
Earl of Pembroke and Montgomery.
Earl Stanhope.
Earl Cairns.

Lord Tyrone.
Lord Carysfort.
Lord Kenry.
Lord Brabourne.

The EARL CAIRNS in the Chair.

Order of adjournment read.

The Proceedings of the Committee of Monday last are read.

The following Witnesses are called in, and examined, viz., Mr. *George Hill Smith* and Mr. *William Henry Gray* (*vide* the Evidence).

Ordered, That the Committee be adjourned till Friday, the 6th of July, at Eleven o'clock.

Die Veneris, 6° Julii 1883.

LORDS PRESENT:

Marquess of Salisbury.
Earl of Pembroke and Montgomery.
Earl Stanhope.

Earl Cairns.
Lord Tyrone.
Lord Brabourne.

The EARL CAIRNS in the Chair.

Order of adjournment read.

The Proceedings of the Committee of Friday, the 1st of June, are read.

The following Witness is called in, and examined, viz., The *O'Conor Don* (*vide* the Evidence).

A DRAFT REPORT is laid before the Committee, and is agreed to (*vide* the Report).

Ordered, That the Lord in the Chair do make the said Report to the House.

MINUTES OF EVIDENCE.

LIST OF WITNESSES.

Die Veneris, 1° Junii, 1883.

Mr. George Hill Smith . . . . .
Mr. William Henry Gray . . . . .

Die Veneris, 6° Julii, 1883.

The O'Conor Don . . . . . .

Die Veneris, 1° Junii, 1883.

Marquess of Salisbury.
Earl of Pembroke and Mont-
  gomery.
Earl Stanhope.
Earl Cairns.

Lord Tyrone.
Lord Castletown.
Lord Kenry.
Lord Braboorne.

THE EARL CAIRNS, IN THE CHAIR.

Mr. GEORGE DILL SMITH, is again called in ; and further Examined, as follows :

1828. [Chairman.] Were you counsel in certain cases that were **heard at Portadown**, before Messrs. Wylie, Smith, and Ferguson, in the month of April last, connected with the estate of Mr. Cope ?
I was. They were heard actually at Armagh, though the decisions were delivered at Portadown.

1829. Was there one of those cases in which a question arose as to the good faith of certain evidence given by the tenant **about his improvements**; his drainage ?
There were altogether six cases, though they were all cases of the one tenant.

1830. What was the tenant's name ?
William Williamson. It is the case where there are separate holdings, and separate rents received for them, that the tenant, though he may have ten different holdings on the same estate, must serve a separate notice for each.

1831. So that there were in this instance six separate cases ?
Six separate cases.

1832. And did the question as to the truth of the evidence about the drainage relate to the whole six, or to one of the holdings ?
To the extent six. I may mention that in the particulars **of the** improvements that were served upon the landlord, and in the evidence **that** was given in Court with reference to them, the tenant sought to sustain a claim for thorough drainage on about 46 acres of land altogether, and, acting as counsel for the landlord, I cross-examined him, as the Court appeared to think rather too severely, with reference to that claim ; and the suggestion was practically made that, with a man of the responsibility of W. Williamson, paying an aggregate rent of nearly 150 l., I was pressing the cross-examination too far. However, I, of course, endeavoured to discharge my duty at the time, and when the Commissioners came to give judgment, the decision that they gave showed that my cross-examination tended exactly **to elicit the truth**. I will read, with your Lordships' permission, the actual **decision** which was pronounced by Mr. Commissioner Wylie.

1833. Before you read it, I should like to ask you from what it is taken ; is it taken from any authentic report ?

(129.)   A 3   No,

No, there are no authentic reports of the Sub-Commissioners' Courts, but what is invariably done is, that the Sub-Commissioner hands the manuscript of the judgment to the reporters of the morning papers who are in Court at the time. I was not present when this particular judgment was delivered myself; I was attending here in London before your Lordship on that day, but I ascertained subsequently that the same rule was adopted in this case, and that what appeared in the "Northern Whig," from which I am going to quote, was printed from Mr. Wylie's own manuscript.

1834. You are going to put in, then, this transcript of the judgment?
I am.   (*The document is handed in, vide Appendix.*)

1835. Have you got a table showing the figures in these six cases of the old rents and the judicial rents?
I have; and that table shows that the judicial rents as fixed are within 3 l. 14 s. 7 d. of what they would be on the arithmetical calculation principle which I submitted to your Lordships the last day that I was here, that is to say, taking the valuation for the tenant, and the valuation for the landlord, merely adding these two together, and dividing in two. The actual judicial rents are 100 l. 12 s. 6 d., and the rents by that arithmetical process would have been 112 l. 7 s. 1 d.; and I may mention with reference to one of these cases, that, practically, the entire deficiency is accounted for in this way; the arithmetical process would bring out 124 l. 11s. 6 d., and the judicial rent actually fixed is 124 l. 5s.; and that is one case in which Mr. Commissioner Wylie gave effect to the last clause of his judgment, where he says, "we have only allowed for such improvements as were plainly visible on inspection." I may mention that in that case, outside of the drains (the evidence in relation to which the Commissioners did not believe at all), the only claim made for improvement was for the removal of a few perches of fence in the year 1847. I would like also to state, as some of the cases upon this estate are mentioned in my previous evidence (I refer to the Cope estate), that the result of the decision in this case of Williamson's, where the evidence was disbelieved, is to give the tenant a reduction of about 16 per cent. upon his old rent, and to make his judicial rent 14 per cent. under Griffith's valuation on land alone, exclusive of buildings, that being a larger reduction than any other tenant on the Cope estate has ever yet got.   (*The document was handed in, vide Appendix.*)

1836. What would have been the result, do you suppose, if his evidence had been believed?
If his evidence had been believed, the judicial rent, I should say, would have been something like 80 l. instead of 100 l.

1837. My question arose from this: his own valuation put the six holdings at 104 l. 12 s. 6 d., and the judicial rent was 100 l. 12 s. 6 d.; so that there was only 4 l. difference?
That is so; it is fair to state that the valuator that was produced for him did not profess to give evidence to his statement about having thorough drained 45 or 46 acres altogether.

1838. Were you counsel in certain cases, on the estate of Mr. Gervais, heard at Clogher, in the county of Tyrone, before Commissioners Ellis and Byers?
I was; those were cases that were heard there while Mr. Sub-Commissioner Foley was over here before your Lordships; in order to prevent there being stagnation in the work of the court, the proceedings on both sides consented to go on with the cases in the presence of the two his colleagues.

1839. It is the lay Commissioners, we understand, who do fix the value?
Yes.

1840. How many cases were there?
There were 14 cases in all upon the estate, and the judicial rents that were fixed amount, on the 14 cases, to 179 l. 5 s., and by the arithmetical process, that is of adding the valuations for the landlord and tenant together, and dividing by two, the judicial rents would have been 180 l. 8 s. 7¼ d., being a difference on the 14 cases of 1 l. 3 s. 7¼ d.

1841. Can you hand in a table **of those?**

I have here the date when the cases were heard, the names of the parties, who did return, and the figures of the valuation, and the rents. I made notations also that I have other cases. Looking at the last statistics I gave, and the fact that they were applicable only to the year 1882, I thought that possibly the question might fairly arise as to whether the same course was being adopted since, and that your Lordships might like to have further evidence upon that point, therefore when I got the instruction to come over and appear again before your Lordships, I thought it well to have out the figures of cases that have been heard since I was here before, and Schedule B. of this table [which] I propose, with your Lordships' approval, to hand [in] contains an analysis of decisions pronounced on the 29th of last month (that is 29 May) in cases on the estate of the Rev. Walter Kidwell, which were heard in Armagh on the 23rd May by Messrs. Wylie, Smith, and Ferguson. There were seven cases on that estate in which the decisions have been pronounced. The judicial rents are 58 l. 2 s. 6 d., in the aggregate, and the arithmetical calculation, by exactly the data proven as that which I have mentioned already, is 67 l. 4 s. 9 d., showing a discrepancy on the seven cases of 17 s. 9 d.

1842. Then you put in that table also?

Certainly. *The documents are handed in, vide appendix.* Then I have added another table of cases heard before Mr. Foley's Sub-Commission at Cookstown on the 15th of May, the decisions in which were pronounced on the 29th May; those are cases on the estate of Mr. Charles G. B. Kennedy, and in those cases, of which there are eight in all, the total of the judicial rents amounts to 140 l. 9 s., and the arithmetical calculation process would make it 154 l. 12 s. 6 d., being a difference there of 5 l. 3 s. 6 d., but it is curious that in two of these cases the judicial rents have been fixed at figures lower than the tenant's valuer's figures of the estimate of the land.

1843. Earl Tyrone.] In the judgment you were mentioning just **now, the legal Commissioner,** I think, said on this question of false drainage that **it was of** rare occurrence?

He did.

1844. Have you any idea as **to how he could know whether it was a rare** occurrence or not?

I think myself that the only rare occurrence **about the matter is to find a Commissioner** bold enough to make such a statement **as that in court.** I am satisfied that the occurrence is not rare.

1845. Lord *Brabourne.*] The detection of it may be rare, you think?

Or even the detection of it; but the expression of the opinion of the Commissioners that they have detected it is exceedingly rare.

1846. Lord Tyrone.] Do you think, with your knowledge **of the way in** which they examine the holdings, that they may very easily be **humbugged as** regards these drains?

There is no doubt whatever about it. Take lands inspected on these holdings where crops are coming up, it is a physical impossibility to ascertain whether drains exist in the places where the tenants say they are; and it is impossible almost to say whether the crop upon the ground is the result of the land being drained, or whether it is due only to the quality of the soil. As a matter of fact, the Commissioners do not make very strict inquiries as to the situation of the drains, except, I suppose, in those particular cases in which their attention has been directed to it in cross-examination. A tenant points out the opening of a drain; and he says, for example, that that is a drain which extends 160 perches in that direction; and if it appears to be an opening that is fairly working, and the land capable of being drained, I think the Commissioners take it, as a matter of course that the drain is there.

1847. Therefore I suppose, although the legal Sub-Commissioner stated that it was a rare occurrence, you know that it might have happened very often and not been detected?

I am quite sure of it, but it was of such an extensive character in this case that I suppose they felt bound to take some notice of it in Court.

1848. Were you concerned in a case of Chaine v. Nelson?

No, I was not in that case myself; but that was a case that decided the question of when the judicial rent was to be held to accrue due from. The Land Commissioners at their original sittings issued a pamphlet in which the subject was dealt with, and two or three times made from the bench a statement not connected with cases that were before them; but as a sort of extra-judicial utterance, to the effect that the 60th section of the Act bore upon applications to fix fair rents, and that the result of that section was that when the fair rent was fixed in a "recorded" case, no matter how long after the Act came into operation, it related back to the gale day immediately after the passing of the Act. Chaine v. Nelson was a case in which Mr. Chaine, one of the Bye-laws for county Antrim, brought an action against a tenant of his, who had had a judicial rent fixed prior to November 1882. The next instant was for a year's rent from the judicial, but the old rent, from November 1881 to November 1882. The distinction taken in that was the judgment in Court of the amount of the judicial rent, and pending the order of the Land Court, as an answer to the remainder of the amount. The action came so far still in the last assizes before Chief Baron Palles, in Belfast, and that learned judge expressed no doubt as to the construction of the 60th section; but when it was mentioned to him that it was a case that would affect some £40,000 or £50,000 tenants perhaps, and he was asked to state a case for the consideration of the full Court of Common Pleas, out of which the writ had issued, he said that he would do so. That was the case that came before the Court of Common Pleas recently, and they ruled that the section had no bearing on an application to fix a fair rent, because all its terms were exhausted by being applied to the 19th section, which deals with eviction cases. I may mention that since that decision, the Land Commission Court itself has issued a circular, and I would ask permission just to hand in a copy of that circular, which is in these terms: "The view of the Irish Land Commissioners on this subject has been, that when an application, grounded on the tenant's originating notice to fix a fair rent, was moved in Court, on the first adjournment of the sitting of the Court, and stood adjourned, the case came within the provisions of the 60th section of the Land Law Act, and that the order made thereon, fixing the fair rent, had the same effect as if it had been made on the day when the Act came into force. Under this construction of the statute, the judicial rent would begin to accrue due in such a case from the gale-day next succeeding the passing of the Act (22nd August 1881). The Common Pleas Division of the High Court of Justice has, however, now decided that the 60th section has not the effect above mentioned, and that the judicial rent in every case begins to accrue due from the gale-day next after the actual decision fixing such rent, and not earlier." I may also mention that since the issue of that circular, I have myself applied to two bodies of Sub-Commissioners to carry the form of the order which they have been using up to the present time, and which in recorded cases, relates the 60th section, and declares that the rent is only payable, or that it is payable, from the gale-day subsequent to the passing of the Act. Both sets of Sub-Commissioners declined to make any alteration in the order, on the very fair ground that they had got no communication from head quarters to justify them in altering the form supplied to them.

1849. Chairman.] What is the 60th section?

It provides that a tenant entitled to make any application under the Act, making it on the occasion of the first sitting of the Court, shall be held to have made the application immediately after the passing of the Act, and that any order made upon it shall operate as if it had been made immediately after the passing of the Act.

1850. Marquess of Salisbury.] I think you said that the Chief Commissioners had issued a circular?

They have, and I have read it.

1851. How

1851. How is it then that the Sub-Commissioners have not received it ?
The circular has been issued by the Chief Commissioners as a leaflet, and sent to all the newspapers and published, but they have made no formal communication of it to the Sub-Commissioners to authorise them to change the forms which are supplied to them for their orders.

1852. To whom do you imagine then the circular is addressed, to the general public or to the Sub-Commissioners ?
To the general public.

1853. It has been kept from the official knowledge of the Sub-Commissioners altogether ?
They have had no copy of it sent to them with any direction or leave to alter the printed forms of orders that have been supplied to them.

1854. They decline to take judicial notice of any communications which the Chief Commissioners may make to the newspapers ?
Certainly. There is one other matter that I wish to place before your Lordships. On the last occasion I was here, I think I mentioned the course adopted at the hearing of appeals with reference to the Court Valuer's figures; I had not then with me anything except the ordinary printed form of the list of Appeals. That I handed to your Lordships, and I find that it has been printed in the Appendix. I now ask the Committee to allow this list to go in also, or to be substituted for the other one. This is a copy of the appeal list actually used at Omagh on the 16th of last month, and, having transcribed it myself from the official copy I have put the figures of the Court Valuer's Report in each case, in the place which they occupy in the copies that are furnished to the Head Court and to the registrar. Thus list will exactly show your Lordships how the matter stands. The column in which the registrar puts the figures of the official Valuer's Report, for the guidance of the Court of Appeal, was blank in the copy I handed in. The copy I now hand in contains the actual figures, in the case of those appeals that were heard at Omagh on the 16th of May. (The document is handed in, vide Appendix.)

1855. Lord Tyrone.] Have you heard of any other principle except the arithmetical calculation, which you have suggested, being adopted ?
I recollect reading in a newspaper, I think, in the early part of last year, a statement purporting to be the report of a speech made by Mr. William Gray, who was, I think, subsequently, for a short time a Sub-Commissioner.

1856. Is that Mr. Gray the Court Valuer?
No, the gentleman I refer to was appointed and acted. I think, for a short time, as a Sub-Commissioner ; I do not know whether he is acting as a Sub-Commissioner now or not. According to the report in the paper of his speech the principle that he purported to enunciate was to take the Government valuation of the land ; find out what the taxes affecting the land in that particular locality were ; deduct the amount of taxes from the Government valuation ; divide the residue by two, and give the one half to the landlord, and the other half to the tenant.

1857. Chairman.] You have not any authentic report of that statement, have you ?
No, nothing except the newspaper report.

1858. Lord Brabourne.] May I ask you whether those are the words to which you refer ?
I can only speak from recollection.

1859. This is a quotation from the "Morning News" of 17th January 1882. "I may be asked what standard would I propose for fixing rents. My reply would be : take the valuation (if we must take valuations), deduct the taxes, and the half would be a fair rent. For instance, if Griffith's valuation of a farm be 20 s. per acre, and the taxes say, 3 s., then 8 s. 6 d per acre would be a fair rent ; a rent that would not encroach on the tenant's improvements. But I am not certain that when the forces represented by steam and the contemplated arrangements in America are fully carried out and developed, that even this will not be an exorbitant rent, in the face of the competition; the farmer will

have to contend with. And notwithstanding the howl of distress that was given vent to at a meeting in Dublin, landlords would, at 8 s. 6 d. per acre, have plenty to live on; indeed, as much as is good for them." Are those the words?
I would not undertake to say that those are the exact words of a speech that was made 12 or 14 months ago, but that is the purport of them. I think that gentleman was not appointed a Sub-Commissioner until some months after that.

1860. I should like to supplement that by another question. I do not know that it was in the same speech, I think it was later in the same year that the same gentlemen is reported to have made this statement; "They" (the farmers) " would not, however, give up agitation, and before 1691 they would have another Act which would be a greater improvement on the Act of 1881 than the Act of 1881 was on that of 1870"?
I did not see that at all. There is just one other matter; I ask permission to hand in, in connection with the appeal list, which I have handed in at Omagh, an analysis which I have made of the result of the operation of the Appeal Court upon those cases; and after sectionalizing the different estates, the summary of the cases that were heard resolves itself into this: The judicial rents that were fixed by the Sub-Commissioners amounted to 595 l. 10 s.; that figure was made 412 l. 10 s., as the result of appeal. In the cases which were so dealt with, the Court Valuer's estimate of the value of the holdings represents 517 l. 3 s. 9 d., and the observation made at the end of 13 reports out of 28, was that as the figure given the tenant would still have a substantial interest in his holding. I have therefore added this note, "besides leaving the tenants a substantial interest in their holdings, the Court has deducted from their own Court Valuer's estimate of a fair rent for ' improvements ' (already taken into account in the 'substantial interest' of each tenant) about 20 per cent." The only alteration is an alteration of 17 l., as the result of the appeals in those particular 28 cases.

The Witness is directed to withdraw.

[Errata.—The Witness desires to state that the name of the landlord given by him in answer to Question 447 (on page 48 of Third Report, and at head of page 101 in Appendix thereto) should have been Earl of " Caledon " instead of Earl of " Gosford." —C. H. S.]

Mr. WILLIAM HENRY GRAY, is called in; and Examined, as follows:

1861. Chairman.] YOU are an extensive farmer in the county of Westmeath, are you not?
I am.

1862. How much land do you farm there?
Nearly 700 statute acres.

1863. Do you hold that as tenant or as owner?
In both ways.

1864. And what you farm you farm yourself?
I farm 700 acres in my own hands.

1865. And you are a magistrate, I think, of the county?
I am.

1866. For how many years have you been a magistrate?
For 25 years; since June 1858, I think.

1867. You have been largely employed, have you not, as a land valuer?
I have, in a good many counties.

1868. And after the Land Act passed, you practised, did you not, as a valuer before the Commission Courts?
I have; in January 1882 I commenced, and have been employed so ever since.

1869. What

1869. What were the Sub-Commissions you appeared before chiefly ?
Mr. Kane's Sub-Commission in Kildare, King's and Queen's Counties. At the time I commenced his circuit was Kildare, King's and Queen's Counties.

1870. Are there any other Sub-Commissions that you practise before ?
Mr. Foley's Sub-Commission.

1871. Any other ?
Mr. Crean's ; I am speaking previous to my appointment as official valuer.

1872. Before any of those Sub-Commissions has your attention been called at all to any arithmetical principle or process which would account for the way in which the reduced rents were fixed ?
My attention has been called to that.

1873. What did you find to be the case ?
I found that in some cases they were the mean between the landlord's value and the tenant's value.

1874. You mean the judicial rent ?
The judicial rent ; I have a memorandum here that was sent to me by the agent of a property, or handed to me last July. It is the case of the Reverend Mr. Scott, in the county of Meath.

1875. Is it a document as to the accuracy of which you are able to judge yourself ?
Yes.

1876. What does it state ?
There were five cases. It gives the old rent in one column, the date when the old rent was fixed in another column, the Poor Law valuation in another, the tenant's valuation in another, the landlord's valuation in another, the mean between the two, and the judicial rent. (*The document is handed in, vide Appendix*).

1877. There are five cases mentioned here : the aggregate of the old rent is 463 *l.* 9 *s.* 6 *d.* ; the aggregate of the judicial rent is 389 *l.* 15 *s.*, and the mean, on the principle mentioned between the two valuations, 386 *l.* 3 *s.* 3 *d.*, a difference of 3 *l.* ?
Yes.

1878. Less than one per cent. Is there any other observation that you have to make upon that paper ?
There was a building charge on one holding ; that would, in fact, make the mean clear.

1879. When were you appointed an official valuer ?
In September 1882 ; my appointment commenced the 16th September ; I was appointed for three months.

1880. What Commission were you appointed to in the first instance, Longford and Westmeath, I think ?
Longford and Westmeath was the first ; I never acted on it.

1881. You did not act for that ?
No.

1882. You were transferred to Mr. Kane's Sub-Commission ?
Yes.

1883. Did that comprise Dublin, Kildare, King's and Queen's Counties ?
Yes ; Dublin, Kildare, King's and Queen's Counties.

1884. Were you afterwards transferred to Mr. Reeves' Commission in Clare ?
Yes.

1885. What was the reason of the transfer ?
The reason assigned by the Commissioners was, that Mr. Kane's Sub-Com-

intention, was about setting in King's County, and that I had raised so much previously there, that it would be inconvenient to have me going over the same properties; it was something to that effect. That was the reason assigned, but there were other reasons.

1886. I do not know that we need go into it, but I believe objection was taken publicly to you?
It was.

1887. It was stated that you valued too high or too favourably to the landlords, was it not?
They objected to my valuations in the County Dublin, where we did not find it necessary to lower the rents. Our decisions were upheld on appeal.

1888. Your decisions were confirmed on appeal?
They were, and some of the rents were even raised.

1889. Did you receive any instructions from the Chief Commissioners on your appointment?
There was a printed paper; I cannot call them instructions; just saying that there was to be an official valuer attached to each Commission, saying also that it was my duty to go out with the Sub-Commissioners and lend the same and give him all the assistance I could in coming to a proper conclusion as to the value of the holding. They did not give me any instructions as to how to value.

1890. No principles as to how to value were laid down?
No, not at all.

1891. Did you find in your experience of the Sub-Commissions that the different Sub-Commissions were proceeding upon any uniform principle as to valuation?
They were not.

1892. So far as you can judge, that is to say?
Some of them I could not understand at all. Does your Lordship speak of while I was official valuer?

1893. Yes?
On the two Sub-Commissions (Mr. Kane's and Mr. Reeves') there was a difference.

1894. And did they proceed upon any uniform principle, or upon any principle at all?
On Mr. Kane's Commission we valued the land as we found it, and we allowed for landlords' improvements and for tenants' improvements, and the cost of buildings, if assented to by the landlord; in that case we added a percentage (what we thought fair) to the rent. If they were the tenant's buildings we took no notice of them. On Mr. Kane's Sub-Commission we disregarded the buildings where they were the tenant's.

1895. You took no notice of them?
No, they were the tenant's property and we did not value them; we valued the land as we found it. We deducted both for landlord's and tenant's improvements on the land.

1896. I do not quite understand you?
We balanced the improvements account both sides, if there happened to be any; and of buildings if they were the tenant's we took no notice. We did not alter our valuation at all except in the cases where the buildings were the landlord's. We then added to the value of that tenant.

1897. What was the principle on which you proceeded on Mr. Reeves' Commission?
So far it was the same, except that when the buildings were the tenant's, we deducted, as part of the improvements, a sum from the value of the land.

[Signed. Earl]

1898. Earl of *Pembroke and Montgomery.*] Having first assessed rent upon them?
Yes.

1899. So that it came to the same thing, did it not?
Practically, on Mr. Reeves' Sub-Commission it would be the value of the tenant's buildings, less than it would be on Mr. Kane's.

1900. *Chairman.*] I do not quite understand that. Speaking now of Mr. Reeves' Sub-Commission, do you mean to say that you valued the land, with the buildings on it, as if it were going, in the first place, to be let to a new man, an incoming tenant; is that what you mean?
No, we valued the land.

1901. Without the buildings?
Without the buildings; at least I did.

1902. What did you do next?
The improvements on either side we added or deducted, according to the side they belonged to.

1903. That is to say, if they were improvements made by the landlord you added them?
We added them; if they were improvements by the tenant we deducted them.

1904. I do not understand how you valued the land in the first instance without the improvements?
We valued the land as we found it in the first instance.

1905. Did you find it with the improvements on it?
We did; we made a deduction then for the tenant's improvements, if he had made drainage or anything of that sort.

1906. You must first have valued the land with the improvements?
Certainly.

1907. With all the improvements, no matter who made them?
No matter who made them.

1908. Then if on the evidence you found that the tenant had made certain improvements, you made a deduction in respect of those improvements?
Yes.

1909. But I take it for granted that if you found the landlord had made the improvements, you did not do anything at all in the way of adding or deducting, did you?
I cannot speak certainly about that, for the landlords have done very little in the way of improvements down in Clare.

1910. If you had added them then you see you would have included them twice over. You say you first valued the land as you found it, with all the improvements on it?
Yes.

1911. If some of those improvements were the tenant's, probably the right course was to make a deduction in respect of them?
Yes.

1912. But if they were the landlord's you did not make any addition, did you?
No, we did not make any addition.

1913. Then what was the point of difference between Mr. Reeves and the other Sub-Commission?
The buildings.

1914. What was that difference, exactly?
On Mr. Reeves' Commission, if the buildings were executed by the tenant, we deducted

deducted from the rent. We took no notice of them whatever on Mr. Kane's Sub-Commission.

1915. No notice either way?
Neither way, except that on Mr. Kane's, where they were the landlord's improvements, we added them.

1916. You added in the original valuation?
We added to the original valuation.

1917. But in the other case (Mr. Reeves') you did not value the buildings at all, or add anything for the buildings in your valuation, and you did not make any deduction in respect of them afterwards?
We deducted the buildings in the case where they belonged to the tenant; this still tended to lower his rent.

1918. Did you accompany the Sub-Commissioners in their inspection, or did you value by yourself?
I accompanied one of them in every case.

1919. Did the two not go?
No, under the system existing then, one of the Sub-Commissioners sat in Court and heard the cases; when his time came to go out on the land I went with him; I was out every day.

1920. Marquess of Salisbury.] Were there only two lay Sub-Commissioners then working together at that time?
That is all.

1921. Then, as I understand, the practice was this: that the lay Sub-Commissioners sat and heard the evidence one day and went out with you upon the land the next day?
Exactly; it might not be exactly the following day; he might sit two days.

1922. And I presume that his report, whatever it was, was practically the decision of the Court?
On Mr. Reeves' Commission I may say that it was.

1923. If the other Commissioner neither heard the evidence nor inspected the land, did he take any part in the decision?
He had nothing to say to the case at all.

1924. Therefore it was only the one Sub-Commissioner who decided?
That is all, and myself.

1925. Chairman.] Were you accompanied, when you went over the land, by the tenant, or landlord, or their agents?
In Clare and Limerick we very often had no representative of the landlord with us at all, nor had we a map of the farm. We were then completely at the mercy of the tenants, and they could show us where they liked.

1926. You had the tenant go with you?
We had the tenant going with us.

1927. And making any statement he thought fit?
Yes.

1928. Lord Brabourne.] Could you test those statements on the spot?
I did not mind them at all.

1929. But you could test the truth of the statements on the spot, could you not?
Not as to the boundaries of the farm; we had no map.

1930. Did you have many cases of difficulty arising out of drainage?
It is a very hard thing to know whether drainage is done or not, particularly if the land has been cultivated over the thorough drainage; under such circumstances we could not see it. We could see the outfall.

1931. It would be impossible, would it not, to know the extent of the drainage?
It would be impossible to know the extent correctly. At the outfall there might be a discharge of water, and the drain probably might not go 20 yards.

1932. Did you ever test it?
We never had time.

1933. Marquess of Salisbury.] You never opened the drain at all?
Never.

1934. So that absolutely you relied upon the tenant's evidence alone?
The Sub-Commissioner that was with me relied upon what he heard in Court.

1935. Lord Brabourne.] So that if the tenant had made a false outfall, that is to say an outfall which really had no drain attached to it, he would be getting an allowance to which he was not entitled?
He would, if it had not been disproved in Court.

1936. And that may have been the case, so far as you know, in many instances?
It is possible.

1937. Marquess of Salisbury.] It might have been a real outfall, and there might have been a drain of 20 yards, and the tenant could have said that it was 400 yards; you have no way of determining between the two?
Certainly not.

1938. Lord Brabourne.] If the tenant had made a good and proper drain which had lasted for some 30 years say, would not he in all probability have been re-couped his expenditure by the additional fertility of the land?
Certainly.

1939. Then if in addition to that he afterwards got his first expense allowed in the rent, he would be paid twice over, would he not?
He would. As well as I recollect, where the drainage had been, as your Lordship says, 20 years in existence, I do not think we took it much into account.

1940. Had you in your mind any period after which you would not take it into account?
I thought that after they had 20 years use out of it, it was time to make no allowance for it.

1941. Marquess of Salisbury.] And for the date, did you trust to the tenants' evidence alone?
I never heard a word of the tenants' evidence in Court; I never was in Court; I was obliged to trust to my colleague who was out with me upon the land.

1942. Chairman.] How was your colleague, who had heard the evidence in Court, able to apply the evidence to the land without having some verbal statements made to him on the spot?
He had no way of doing it. A very gross case occurred in the County Dublin. The tenant had a very elaborate map made of his farm. It was a very large farm. He had nearly every field laid out in thorough drainage; the map was beautifully made, and when Colonel Bayly and I went on the land he had this map, and he had the man who drew the map (he was the tenant's valuer); we went over some of the fields and we took the map, and we asked him, "where is that outfall" (we could see by the map where it ought to be), and he was not able to show us. In fact he was not able to show us a drain on the whole place.

1943. Lord Brabourne.] If that map had been produced in Court there would have been no means of finding out the mistake, would there?
I was not in Court, but I understand that it was produced. That map was what drew our attention to the matter, and induced us to look for the drains.

1944. *Chairman.*] That tenant had made a map and put down all the particulars upon it; but supposing he had not done that and had given general evidence upon the subject, then the Sub-Commissioner would have had no way of applying that, when he went on the land, except by means of statements made by the tenant, not on oath?
Yes. We asked the valuer, who was some sort of low-class engineer, did he examine the drainage on the field before he made his map, and he said that he did not, but that he took them down in the house from what the tenant told him; he never saw the fields at all.

1945. Marquess of *Salisbury.*] He drew the map in the tenant's room from what the tenant told him?
Exactly.

1946. Did it generally correspond with the outline of the property?
The map was correct enough, and the fields were correct enough, but I am speaking of the drainage. That was a case where the landlord applied on the expiry of the lease to have the rent raised.

1947. Lord *Brabourne.*] But supposing there was perfect honesty and integrity on the part of the tenant, I understand you to say that the time taken to value these farms was hardly sufficient to enable an accurate judgment to be formed as regards drainage?
There was no time at all for testing the drainage.

1948. If you had added to that want of time, dishonesty on the part of the tenant, the impossibility of an accurate estimate being arrived at was very greatly magnified, was it not?
It was in the case of anyone guided by what the tenant would say.

1949. I suppose in Court they would be more or less guided by the tenant's evidence, would they not?
I do not know. I never was in Court. Some people are more disposed to give credit to the tenant than I would be; I am sorry to say, I do not believe all that I am told.

1950. Are valuations going on at this moment on farms?
Yes; I am very largely employed.

1951. Is it possible in the present state of property, and may it not become still more impossible to get upon the land and find where the drains are?
That is so; in fact, except where drainage is recently executed we have no way of knowing anything about it, and even then we have no way of knowing whether it is properly done or not, or what depth it is, unless we have time to test it.

1952. *Chairman.*] Have you seen any collection of prices at which the tenants' interest has been sold since the Land Act was passed?
I have. I have a printed statement here that has been put into my hand, copied from the " Farmers' Gazette."

1953. Of sales since when?
This is a statement of "Sales of farm tenancy under the Irish Land Act, 1881, compiled for and published with 'Farmers' Gazette' of Saturday, 2nd June 1883."

1954. May that be taken, do you think, as an accurate statement?
I believe so. (*The document was handed in, vide Appendix.*) I have here also a copy of the form of the report which the official valuer had to make, if your Lordship would care to see it. (*The document was handed in, vide Appendix.*)

1955. Lord *Tyrone.*] Was the practice different on the two Sub-Commissions of which you have spoken as to your manner of valuing the land?
It was different in respect to the tenants' buildings, decidedly.

1956. But

1956. But as to the information placed at your disposal, was there any difference?
There was a difference there.

1957. In what way?
Of course before I went out, I got the particulars of where I was going, and the farms I had to value, giving me the acreage, the old rent, the poor law valuation, and the tenant's improvements. On Mr. Kane's Sub-Commission, the Sub-Commissioner told me what had been proved in Court as to the improvements by landlord and by tenant; he also told me what the tenant's valuation was, and what the landlord's valuation was. That refers to Mr. Kane's Sub-Commission only. It was not so on Mr. Reeves' Sub-Commission. In that case the Sub-Commissioners always told me that it was against the rules to let me know what occurred in Court at all, as regards the landlord's valuation or the tenant's valuation. They said it was against the rules to compare notes with each other while we were on the land. I was to make an independent valuation without any reference to what they were doing, and they without any reference to what I was doing. It was not so on Mr. Kane's Sub-Commission. We there exchanged ideas on the land, and arrived at what we thought a fair conclusion then and there.

1958. Did the pace at which they examined the holdings differ on the two Sub-Commissions?
Yes.

1959. On which was it the fastest?
On Mr. Reeves'. Sometimes it was very rapid indeed.

1960. Did you find yourself able to fix a fair value, going at the pace you were going?
I did not; I had to go faster than they had; I felt the responsibility upon me; I had to go from one side of the field to another, while they went straight across it, and even in that way I had not the time that I would have liked; I could walk the country just as well as either of them, and I could not keep up with them on some days.

1961. Marquess of Salisbury.] What pace should you give them; three miles an hour?
Well, it was fully that, sometimes. That answer does not apply to every case. Sometimes, true, it may be, did not pass so much.

1962. Lord Tyrone.] But generally, did you consider from their method of examining the land that they were capable of arriving at a fair conclusion as to the value of it?
My opinion is that if they knew as little of the history of the case as I did, and went there as strangers, they could not possibly put a fair value upon the land. What I mean is, that they had heard the case the day before in Court; they knew the case, and every side of it, every bit of it, and I knew nothing at all about it; I was put on the land to walk it and value it while they knew all about it. They had that advantage of me.

1963. Do you consider that with that advantage it was possible for them to arrive at a fair conclusion as to the value?
I say it was not, if they exercised their independent judgment, without knowing more about it. Without knowing what they heard in Court the day before they could not do it.

1964. Have you ever come across tenant's statements that have been told you by the Sub-Commissioners that you could not prove when you were upon the holdings?
I have.

1965. Would not that rather tend to upset the judgment of the Sub-Commissioners, than to assist them?
It would.

1966. Earl Stanhope.] I suppose when tenants have accounts of expenditure, either in drainage or manure to produce, they are called for?
They are, but they are generally speaking very unreliable. Sometimes they do not exist at all; and we cannot see them on the land.

1967. Lord Tyrone.] Do you think it would be an advantage to have maps of the holdings?
Decidedly so. On the practical working of the Act I think there is nothing more wanting than maps. In the south we had very seldom a map, and very often we were for days together without a representative of the landlord upon the land; we might be brought anywhere.

1968. You consider that a map is absolutely necessary to mark the boundaries?
Exactly; that is to say, to test the tenants where the landlord is not represented. Where only one side is represented we should have a map to test the accuracy of the side that is represented.

1969. When you were a Court valuer did you make any deduction for the right of occupation of a tenant?
I did.

1970. How much?
About 15 per cent. Before I became a Court valuer I valued land as if it were in the landlord's hands; that is to say, the letting value of it.

1971. The fair letting value of it?
The fair letting value of it.

1972. And after you became a Court valuer you were obliged to deduct 15 per cent, as I understand?
Yes; and I have adopted that on my private valuations since. I was always asked the question, and I found my former system very inconvenient.

1973. Chairman.] Was this form that you have handed in a form that you used when you were a Court valuer with the Sub-Commission?
Yes, I had to fill up that form.

1974. I see the second head here is "Improvements apparent on the holding"; did you go into any question of who had made the improvements?
We did, in a sort of rather hurried way. Of course, in the case of improvements, I should be guided by what I was told by the lay Commissioners who were with me, for I had not heard the evidence in Court.

1975. Marquess of Salisbury.] There was no representative of the tenant or landlord with you?
Very often there was.

1976. But not always?
Not always.

1977. Lord Tyrone.] Was the method of taking the improvements into consideration rather a haphazard method?
It was.

1978. Was there any measurement, or anything of that sort?
We had no way of measuring. If we had been supplied with an Ordnance map we could have done it, but it would have taken about double or treble the time to go into every little detail.

1979. On Mr. Reeves' Commission, did you come upon any cases in which deductions were made for internal fencing?
Yes.

1980. Was it the usual practice to do so?
It was, I believe. I have had to do it myself by the direction of Mr. Reeves or the direction of the Sub-Commissioners.

1981. Was

1981. Was it usual on that Commission to value the buildings and deduct them from the value of the land?
Yes, it was, where they were the tenant's.

1982. I think I understood you to say just now that the landlord was often not represented at the inspection of a farm?
Very often. It so happened on some occasions that neither landlord nor tenant was represented, and we had to poke our way to find the farm and get someone about there to show it to us.

1983. Marquess of Salisbury.] Are you sure that you never valued the wrong one?
I could not tell.

1984. Lord Tyrone.] Is it difficult to get particulars of improvements from the tenants?
It is difficult to get correct particulars. They give a very long elaborate bill of improvements, which, in most cases, are not found correct.

1985. And are they often a good deal exaggerated?
Very often; generally so. Of course that does not apply to every case. Some of them are honestly given in.

1986. In reply to question 231, Mr. Reeves appears to have made this statement, "The duty of the official valuer was to accompany on the land one Assistant Commissioner who had sat with him and heard the evidence;" probably the word "him" is a mis-print, and should be "me;" I understand from you that you did not hear the evidence?
I never did hear the evidence.

1987. I understand you to say that you never sat with the Lay Sub-Commissioners?
I never sat with them. I walked with them. Mr. Reeves must have intended to convey that it was the Sub-Commissioner who sat with himself, and not that the valuer sat with the Lay Commissioner.

1988. I will read to you the continuation of the answer: "He went over the holding with the Assistant Commissioner, heard the evidence second-hand from him, and then filled up the sheet"?
That is it exactly.

1989. Have you a table of some small reductions that have been made in the County Limerick?
Yes.—(The Document is handed in, vide Appendix.)

1990. From your experience in acting as valuer, is it your opinion that the reductions have increased of late, or not?
On some Sub-Commissions they have; there is something given to the tenant. That is my opinion; in fact, in every case that goes into Court, whether right or wrong, the tenant gets more or less, from what I have seen.

1991. He always gets a reduction, or almost always?
Almost always, except that there might be one case out of ten or 20 on a property in which he would not get a reduction.

1992. Do you think it is a satisfactory system, to appoint Sub-Commissioners for a limited time?
I think it is not.

1993. Why do you think so?
I do not think they can act altogether independently; that is, taking the generality of human nature; public pressure is on them.

1994. You think that public pressure is brought to bear upon them?
It is; I do not think it is possible for a set of men that wish to keep quiet and retain their position to act independently. There are cases of course where

(139.)   C   they

they do not; there are some independent men amongst them; I know some of them; they do not like to be brought before the public in any way; for example, by questions asked in the House of Commons, and so on.

1995. Do you think that the removal of Sub-Commissioners from different districts, in consequence of agitation, has had a bad effect as regards the increase of the reductions?

I take it that it is a sort of notice to the other Sub-Commissioners, that if they do not act in a certain way they also will be hunted about.

1996. You yourself were removed, I think, on two or three occasions?

I was, I may say, on only one occasion, because my first appointment was a wrong one. They appointed me to my own county. That was just a mistake, and it was cancelled by telegram the day I got the appointment.

1997. You were removed after Lord Talbot de Malahide's cases were heard, were you not?

Not altogether after that; there were some cases to be heard at Edendery where they alleged that I had valued, and where I never valued at all; it was my namesake who valued there.

1998. Marquess of *Salisbury*.] You were removed for the valuations of your namesake?

I was.

1999. Lord *Tyrone*.] The improvements which the tenants claim against, we have been told, mainly of drainage, hedges, buildings, and reclamations; is not that the case?

That is generally the case.

2000. I wish to ask you with respect to reclamation, were you called upon when the tenant pretended to have reclaimed, to value the land that his reclamation had added to the holding?

We were.

2001. You could only do that by comparing the state of the ground as it existed before reclamation, with the state of the ground as it existed after, could you?

Yes, that is to say the state of the ground which we never saw.

2002. How did you contrive to do that sum without seeing one side of the calculation?

It was more haphazard than anything else. I always refused as much as I could to do it myself without seeing both sides.

2003. You had no evidence laid before you as to the state in which the ground had been prior to its reclamation, had you?

No, unless we saw some similar ground unreclaimed adjoining such as cut away bog.

2004. That would no doubt be a guide to some extent, but in the absence of such a guide you would have none?

None.

2005. You could only give a general guess as to what the herenum was likely to be?

That is all.

2006. Were you ever asked to value a farm to which injury had been done by the bad husbandry of the tenant?

I never was asked to do it.

2007. Was it ever suggested to you?

I do not say it has been suggested to me, but we have found farms evidently injured by the neglect of the tenant.

2008. Had you to value what you esteemed to be an injury done to the holding by bad husbandry on the tenant's part?

Yes,

You, particularly in the case of drainage. Where the drains were choked by neglect, and the want of efficient drainage was injuring the land, we valued the land, I always did, the land and the drains were kept in order.

2009. And their added to the rent in consequence?
I put a higher value upon the lands, and treated them as if they were to be permanently in that state. Tenants sometimes get their farms ready for inspection. I have seen water let in on land before I have gone upon it.

2010. And have you seen any other kind of preparation for this **visit of the Commissioners?**
Yes: I have seen this, which is a very good thing for the tenant; he will run over his grips, and open the mouths of his thorough drainage for inspection where he has claimed improvements for drainage. He may clear the neglect of years probably and open the whole thing, to show that he has done the improvement.

2011. I suppose that improvement only extends to that part of the drain or other work which is open to the eyes of the valuer?
Yes.

2012. How could you tell that the drain was running. You could only do it by seeing water flow through it?
That is all.

2013. Supposing it was dry weather, how did you tell?
We had no way of knowing it accurately.

2014. You assumed that a drain was good if the tenant told you that it was?
I did not, though it was expected that we would do so.

2015. You had no means of proving the contrary, had you?
No, if I went on land where the tenant said he had drained it, and I found it wet, and that it wanted draining, I would judge then that he had not drained it.

2016. With regard to reclamations, had you any reclamation to value which consisted in removing stones from the land?
We had some in Clare.

2017. When that had been done at a distant date, did you value the reclamation at the price the same would cost at the present day?
No, I did not.

2018. You would allow for the difference of times and circumstances?
I would.

2019. Were there many reclamations of that kind placed?
There was a good deal claimed for removing stones in Clare. Half the country there is what we call "crag." Of course I never saw the land before the stones were removed. I may have seen the walls that were built, and I may have seen the pits that the stones were taken out of, or something of that kind, and made a rough guess.

2020. With respect to good husbandry, I suppose you **did not expect of a** tenant that he should manure the land?
I think he should manure it; I never allowed anything for manuring.

2021. Did a case ever come before you of a holding which had been given to the tenant in a highly cultivated condition, and which he by neglect had reduced in value, which he had recouped at the present day?
I suppose it has, but I did not see the land in the original condition. I would take what I was told as to the condition in which it was when he got it.

2022. You had no security for giving effect to that?
I value the land as I find it.

2023. Then of course you would value it at the lower rent which would be

attributable to it in the state to which he had reduced it, and not at the higher
rent attributable to the state in which he had received it ?
Unless it was admitted that it was in a better state of cultivation when he
got it.

2024. As a matter of fact you had no means of testing anything historical
with regard to the farms; you had only what was before your eyes?
That is so; I never sat in court, I was the official valuer.

2025. Lord Brabourne.] I suppose it is not easy to tell what state it may
have been in at the time the occupation commenced?
No; there are some tenants who have occupied the holdings from one genera-
tion to another.

2026. Does not the cursory nature of the visits of the Sub-Commissioners
afford a great temptation to tenants to practise deceit?
Certainly.

2027. If you detected a tenant attempting to deceive, did you take measures
to make it known to the Court that was going to decide the rent?
Yes, I was not always present when the rents were being fixed. Just immediately before the judgments were given I was probably in another part of the
country, and the Commissioners had only my reports.

2028. What I mean is this. Suppose you were looking over a farm with
your colleague, and you found that the tenant with regard to drains or reclamation, or what not, was evidently trying to deceive you, did you leave it entirely
to your colleague to represent that to the Court, or did you yourself make it
your business to bring it to the notice of the Commissioners?
In my report there is a place for "tenants' improvements," and I would say
"none." That would meet that case.

2029. Would you specify that he had alleged improvements which did not
exist?
My report would state that there were no improvements apparent.

2030. That is not quite the question. You might state that there were no
improvements apparent, but of course if you stated that he had alleged improvements, and that they did not exist, and you brought it to the mind of the
Commissioners, that would throw a great doubt over his evidence on all points,
would it not?
Of course it would.

2031. Did you do that?
My report saying that there were no apparent improvements, and my colleague having heard evidence that there was, I conceived that my report was a
direct contradiction of that evidence.

2032. Did I understand you to say that you compared notes sometimes, or
that you did not compare notes with the Sub-Commissioner who was with you
upon the land?
Upon Mr. Kane's Sub-Commission, I did; generally speaking I did so with
both men, Colonel Bayley and Mr. Barry.

2033. Were the Sub-Commissioners who were with you practical valuers, like
yourself?
They were. Mr. Barry, I believe, was agent to Lord Emly; he farms largely
himself.

2034. But, as a matter of fact, have you found much difference of opinion
between yourself and these gentlemen, or did you correspond?
Very little difference indeed; I do not suppose there was one and a half per
cent. between my valuation and theirs in the whole of the cases put together
over the three counties.

2035. Earl Stanhope.] Did you take a field-to-field valuation, or did you
make a valuation of the whole farm generally?
Do you mean when I was official valuer?

2036. When

2036. When you went over the land, did you give field-to-field values?
When valuing for landlords privately I did so.

2037. Did you not do so when you valued for a Sub-Commission?
I very seldom had a field-survey, and the quantities were generally taken by our eyes. It may be that we had three or four classes of land on the one holding; in that case we were obliged to do the best we could, and as we had no maps, there was no other way of doing it.

2038. I suppose you had the Government survey maps to guide you, had you not?
We never had.

2039. Then you had no plans?
We had no plans, and we were obliged to use our judgment in saying there are so many acres here at a certain price, and so many there at another price, and so on. That is while I was an official valuer.

2040. Lord Fredericks.] I was going to ask you this: I understand that you were obliged to value these lands, owing to the conduct of your colleagues as regards the hurried way in which the work was done, in a manner much more rapid than you would have done if you had been sent by a private individual to make a fair valuation upon your own reputation?
Precisely so, especially as regards Mr. Reeves' Sub-Commission. In addition to the fact that we had no maps by which to test our quantities, the land would vary very much in quality on the one farm.

2041. It would have been much better, would it not, if, before any valuation was made, reliable maps had been furnished?
Certainly. The want of maps is a very great blot upon the whole system.

2042. Do you not think that greater satisfaction would have been given to the country if that had been done, even if more time had been consumed; that is to say, if the valuations had been made upon such maps, and by independent valuers appointed by the Government?
I believe so.

2043. Earl Stanhope.] In valuing a farm, say of 200 acres, you are told that 150 acres is grass land and the remainder arable, but you are told that, and that is all that you know about it?
Yes, that is all we know about it.

2044. Then you are told that of the 50 acres of arable land half is light land and the other half is heavy land; that you have to take in the same way, do you not?
I never took what I was told; I used my own judgment, generally speaking.

2045. As to the quality of the land, you mean?
As to the different areas and the different qualities.

2046. But not as to the actual acreage; you did not test the acreage at all, did you?
I had no way of testing it; generally, or at all events very often, the inferior land was represented by the tenants as being double the acreage that it actually was, and the quantity of good land was always represented as being very small, and we were obliged to use our judgment.

2047. Lord Tyrone.] The acreage of the good land is always very small, according to the tenant's statement, I understand you to represent?
Yes.

2048. You say also that your valuation and your colleague's valuation were very much the same?
That is on Mr. Kane's Commission.

2049. On the other Commission, was it so?
Mine was about 5 per cent. or better than 5 per cent. over theirs, taking them all round.

2030. Did your valuations at all agree with the judicial rents on the second Commission?
Sometimes.

2031. Did they vary very much on many occasions?
On nearly all. I should say that I was fully 5 per cent. higher than they on the Southern Commission.

2032. Lord *Brabourne*.] Did they vary always in the same direction, higher than the judicial rents?
Almost always, but sometimes (in some few cases) I was below them, I should say.

2033. Lord *Tyrone*.] But, as a rule, you were above theirs, were you not?
As a rule, I was about 4 per cent., or better than 5 per cent., above them.

2034. Earl of *Pembroke and Montgomery*.] Did you value on the same principle that you would have done if there had been no Land Act in existence?
Except as regards the deduction of 15 per cent. that I have stated for occupation, I did.

2035. You valued on the principle of what a solvent tenant could afford to give for the land, I suppose?
Yes.

2036. Lord *Tyrone*.] But you had to knock off in the first instance 15 per cent. for occupation, as I understand?
Yes. I was asked about that question in my own being examined as a witness before my appointment, that I altered my practice as to it. Up to that time I put the letting value on the land, without the 15 per cent. deduction.

2037. Therefore, as I understand you, if you had proceeded upon the principle of putting the fair letting value upon the land, and had done that only, you would have been 15 per cent. above your colleagues?
I would. I was always asked, "What would be the specified value of a holding at the fair letting value?" I say, that it should not be worth anything to a solvent tenant; that is why I put the full letting value on. I say there should be no good-will, or "tenant-right," as they call it in the north.

The Witness is directed to withdraw.

Ordered, That this Committee be adjourned *sine die.*

Die Veneris, 6° Julii, 1883.

LORDS PRESENT:

Marquess of Salisbury.
Earl of Pembroke and Montgomery.

Earl Cairns.
Lord Tyrone.
Lord Brabourne.

THE EARL CAIRNS, IN THE CHAIR.

THE O'CONOR DON, is called in, and Examined, as follows:

3048. (Chairman.) You, as we know, are an extensive Landowner in the South of Ireland?
My property is chiefly in the West of Ireland.

3049. In what county is your property situate?
I have some in Sligo, but the main part of my property is in Roscommon.

3050. Since the passing of the Land Act, have you had any experience of the working of the Clauses relating to the sale of holdings from the landlord to the tenant?
Yes; very shortly after the passing of the Land Act, I endeavoured to carry out a sale of one small townland to some of my tenants. I had some difficulty, I think, about the rents; they complained of the rents being high, and were anxious to go into the Land Court to get their rents fixed, and instead of accepting that, I suggested to them the offer of purchasing, and after a good deal of negotiation we arranged upon terms, under which they would have got a very considerable reduction in their annual payment, considering that as compared to the rent. The facts were simply these; this was an outlying townland that I had purchased about 15 or 20 years before, for the sum of 3,000 l. I had purchased it on a memorial provided to me by the tenants, they undertaking at the time to pay me interest at the rate of about 5 per cent. upon whatever I should have to pay for the Landed Estates Court.

3051. You mean that you made the purchase at the request of the tenants?
I made the purchase at the request of the tenants. It was a condition that I did not agree to buy at all myself. They came in, and pressed me with a memorial begging me to buy, and undertaking to pay interest at the rate of 5 per cent. upon whatever amount I paid for the property. I paid 3,000 l. for it, and subsequently the rent was arranged at 145 l. a year, which was something less than the 5 per cent. It was undoubtedly a high rent, there is no question of that, because I paid a very high price for the property. In January 1881, I came to an arrangement with them to sell this townland to them at 2,400 l.

3052. The same townland?
This very same townland. That was a loss to myself of 600 l., and as most of them were unable to pay one-fourth of the purchase money, I agreed to advance to them one-fourth of the purchase money upon mortgage, which mortgage, of course, as your Lordship is aware, would come second.

3053. Second to the Government charge?
Second to the Government charge. When we had agreed upon this, there were several small charges upon this townland to be arranged for; there was quit

(399.) C 4 quit

quit rent and Crown rent; that was a charge of 16 *s.* 7 *d*: there were lay tithes, I believe, to a neighbouring proprietor (Colonel King-Harman), amounting to about 3 *l.*; there was the ordinary tithe-rent charge, amounting to something about the same sum, between 3 *l.* and 4 *l.*; and there was a drainage charge for a sum of money that I had borrowed under the Board of Works for the improvement of the holdings. According to the first form sent down to me from the Land Commission for the purchase, it was set out that those charges might be apportioned over the tenants, and that it was not necessary to buy them up. Accordingly, this arrangement of sale to them was based upon that assumption, they were to bear a proportion of those charges, and they were not to be paid off.

2065. Then they were to buy for 8,000 *l.*, subject to the charges?
Yes, subject to the charges, with the exception of the drainage charge, and the ordinary tithe-rent charge, both of which I undertook to pay off.

2065. Lord *Brabourne.*] In addition to the loan of your 800 *l.*?
In addition to the loan of my 800 *l.* The capitalised value of the drainage charge, I may state, was 80 *l.* When the forms went up to the Commission, filled in and signed by myself and the tenants, they informed us that they could not assent to the sale unless all the charges were paid off. This, of course, created a great difficulty, because it necessitated a new arrangement with the tenants; and one of these charges (the lay tithe, as it is called, to Colonel King-Harman) was a charge that I could not pay off, because he did not wish to buy it. I do not know whether he would buy it. This was the first difficulty that arose in my carrying out the sale, and after a good deal of correspondence (which I need not point out to your Lordship necessitated legal expense) they consented to allow us, they were obliged to do; they could not help allowing it) this charge of Colonel King-Harman to remain out, but they insisted that the quit and Crown rent should be paid off. They also required that the charge of Colonel King-Harman should be primarily placed upon one holding, and that one tenant should be responsible for the whole of it; and not wishing to break up the arrangement that had gone so far, I consented to it, and with considerable difficulty I got the tenants also to agree to the alterations; new agreements of course had to be drawn out, and the whole matter recast.

2066. *Chairman.*] Was he to have rights of contribution from the other tenants?
His rights remained the same over the whole townland, only that one tenant was primarily liable. Of course so far as Colonel King-Harman is concerned the whole townland is liable still, and each tenant in it is liable. I thought then that the difficulties were all over, and that we should come to a settlement; but I was disappointed even in this, for it was necessary that I should purchase up the quit and Crown rent. The Land Commission did not propose to purchase it up, and my solicitor had to go to the Quit and Crown Rent Office in Dublin for the purpose of purchasing it.

2067. Would you allow me to ask you, before you go on, so that I may follow your observations, whether, when you had purchased these charges up, you were to add the amount that you paid for them to what the tenants were to pay to you?
Yes, the tenants consented to that; I was to add that to them. Then my solicitor went to the Quit and Crown Rent Office for the purpose of purchasing it up, and the rate of purchase demanded for this Government rent (if I may so call it) amounted to between 28 and 30 years' purchase. The sum, of course, was not large, and it did not matter very much; but I confess I thought it a hard thing to have to pay 28 years' purchase when I was selling for about 16; still I did not raise any objection on that score. He then found at the Quit and Crown Rent Office, on examination, that in addition to this sum of 19 *s.* 7 *d.*, which was the charge upon this particular townland called Ardmoile, there was a further sum of 9 *s.* 5½ *d.* which had been a charge upon the town, and was, in fact, a charge upon the townland of Ardmoile, in conjunction with the neighbouring town land called Kerrykeel, which

which belonged to Colonel King-Harman; and although I had never heard of this charge, and although the estate had been sold in the Landed Estates Court without any reference to it, they refused at the Quit and Crown Rent Office to give me a discharge from the rent unless this 9 s. 7 d., which was a charge upon Kerrykeel, was also paid off. Then I was in this position. I could not do that, because it was practically, really and truly, a charge upon an adjoining town land of very considerable value, and a first charge upon it, and was therefore perfectly secure. On the other hand, they said to me, "We will not give you a receipt unless you pay it off;" and I had the Land Commissioners, on the other side, saying, "We will not mention this sale to tenants unless you get a clear receipt from the Quit and Crown Rent Office," so that the business was very nearly breaking up on this question of the 9 s. 7 d.

2068. Twenty-eight times 9 s. 7 d., or about 14 l. ?
Twenty-eight times the 9 s. 7 d. However, I am bound to say that I found the Land Commissioners and their officers all through anxious to facilitate me, so far as they thought they were justified in doing so, and upon representing to them that this town land had been sold to me in the Landed Estates Court without any reference to this 9 s. 7 d., that it was a primary charge upon another town land of very large value, and that it could never come into any practical operation because that town land was primarily responsible for it, they at length consented that they would sanction the sale to my tenant in exactly the same way as the sale had been made to me, without any reference to this 9 s. 7 d.

2069. Would not the conveyance in the Landed Estates Court have barred that 9 s. 7 d. ?
I thought it would, but they said it did not. There was no reference made to it in the conveyance, and there was no statement in the conveyance to the effect that all these rent charges were cleared off.

2070. Lord Brabourne.] Were not the charges upon the estate stated when it was sold to you?
They were not stated in the conveyance; they were stated in the rental that was printed by the Landed Estates Court.

2071. Was this charge stated in that?
No, it was not stated, I think. I was wholly ignorant of it.

2072. Then it comes to this, that the Landed Estates Court sold to you a property with a charge upon it of which they had kept you in ignorance at the time of the sale?
I believe they were quite ignorant of it themselves.

2073. At all events, as the main point, you were ignorant of it?
I was wholly ignorant of it.

2074. Therefore they want to make you now responsible for a subsequent discovery by themselves of a charge which existed at the time of sale, which they did not know of?
Yes, I traced this 9 s. 7 d. back, I may say. The way it arose was this: Sometime about the reign of Queen Elizabeth, the Irish Chieftains to whom the land belonged, entered into the possession of it, paying to the Crown 10 s. Irish currency every quarter for the land. These two townlands of Ardmoile and Kerrykeel were compounded for at that time, and this charge of 10 s. placed equally upon both. Then subsequently, after this was arranged, the sale went on, and within the last few days I have been paid by the Land Commission the amount of the purchase money, so that the sale has been carried out. I saw, in the evidence given before your Lordship, that Colonel King-Harman stated before the Committee that in consequence of those difficulties I had to abandon this attempt. That is not correct; I wanted particularly to call your attention to the fact that trifling as these little difficulties seem, they all heap up costs in these matters of these small sales to tenants.

2075. Chairman.] I think you may consider that you have had a great triumph over all these difficulties?

Yes. While upon that matter of costs, I may mention that I had from a solicitor of very considerable experience in Dublin his table of estimated costs of the sale to four tenants of property worth 800 l.

2076. Is this connected with your sale?
It is not connected with mine.

2077. I was going to ask you, whether you were able to tell us what sort of expenses which you had to pay in the case of your own sales?
The Land Commission costs have not been large. I have not them; they are about 30 l., but the other costs I am not able to state yet. I have here a bill of costs, showing what would be the fair costs of sale in a case of this description, and they amount, upon a transaction of about 800 l. to about 100 l.

2078. In a transaction of about 800 l., the costs amount to that sum?
Yes; the estimate of the costs given to me by a Dublin solicitor, of very considerable experience in these matters, a gentleman who, I believe, has conducted sales in tenants. It is based on the assumption that there is the landlord's solicitor, and the tenant's solicitor, and of course the Land Court solicitor. I may mention that in my own particular case part of this expense was avoided by the fact that the tenants trusted me implicitly in the matter, and employed no solicitor of their own.

2079. Lord Tyrone.] But that expense would be divided between both landlord and tenant, would it not?
Practically the landlord will have to pay it; in my case I had to pay the whole of the costs, that was part of the undertaking. I believe the Land Commission proceed upon the assumption that all costs are to be paid by the landlord. In ordinary cases all stamps and fees upon purchases are paid by the purchaser, but in the particular case of sales under the Land Act these stamps and fees are charged to the seller, to the landlord; I have here a bill which they sent me in for the stamps and fees from the Land Court, and I had to pay these.

2080. Chairman.] What was the amount of the **stamps and fees in your case**?
2 2s. 4 d.

2081. Lord Brabourne.] Could you not have divided them by arrangements with the tenant?
Of course I could have done so if the tenants had chosen to agree, but I do not think they would be likely to agree. Then there is another point that I wish to bring before your Lordships. After this sale is made, and after all these sales are made to the tenants, in cases where money is advanced by the landlord on mortgage, of course there have to be two mortgage deeds. There are, therefore, two sets of mortgages, the mortgage to the Commission and the mortgage to the landlord, and the property is registered in what they call the Registry of Deeds Office in Dublin. All these deeds have to be registered. Memorials have to be drawn up for them, and an immense amount of expense is incurred in that way. I would venture to suggest that, if any other properties should be placed under the Record of Title, these small properties should be placed under the Record of Title. Your Lordship is aware that we have in Ireland two systems of registration, one the Record of Title (which is very like the system adopted under the Act you passed in this country); and the other the old system of registering all the deeds. In all these cases where sales take place to tenants they are not placed on the Record of Title, but under the Registry of Deeds. If it is not attended to, and these purchases go on, I believe that will lead to no end of confusion.

2082. Chairman.] Are you able to give the Committee anything in the nature of an estimate of what the total costs would be in a transaction such as you have described, involving purchase money of 8,000 l., and requiring both a charge in favour of the Government for a portion of the purchase money, history, and a charge in favour of the landlord for the remainder, including the registration?

Only that one which I hold in my hand, which deals with property to the smaller amount of 400 l., but, I believe the costs of sale, in a transaction of 500 l. would be very much the same as in the case of the sum of 2,500 l., with the exception of the stamp duty, the title being simple. In my own case and in this supposititious case I hold in my hand, the titles were both Landed Estates Court titles. When I call this a supposititious case, although I believe the figures are not exactly the same, it is a real case that occurred.

2083. Is there anything else you wish to state upon that subject?
Nothing, beyond my still desiring to call your Lordships' attention to the great importance of the Record of Title being applied to these sales, and if I might, I would ask your Lordship to look into the Report of the Commission that inquired into the registration of deeds in Ireland, about two years ago. In that Report the subject was very much entered into, and there the Record of Title was condemned by the Commission, but condemned upon grounds which I venture to say do not apply at all to these small properties.

2084. Then your view would be that, at all events, in these small properties, it would be better that they should be put on the Record of Title and not free from the Registry of Deeds?
Yes. Of course, on the general principle I have been very strongly in favour of these sales to the occupying tenants, and I believe this to be the only ultimate settlement of the Irish land question. I consider that unless these difficulties, especially the difficulty of dealing with these small payments to the Government, be dealt with, that these sales will turn out to be almost impracticable; and I would suggest with regard to all these public charges, such as quit rent, Crown rent, and title rent-charge, that the Land Commission should purchase them up, and should deal with the other public departments in regard to them, and that there should not be as it were two, what I may call, opposing parties (public departments); because I found no desire whatsoever on the part of the Quit and Crown Rent Office to facilitate the sale or to make any concession whatever.

2085. It is an office that has no connection whatever with the Land Court, is it not?
It has no connection with the Land Court, and although I found the officials of the Land Court most anxious to facilitate the sale, I am bound to say that I did not find the same disposition in the other office. Very naturally they state, it is no business of ours; it is nothing to us whether you sell or not.

2086. Lord Tyrone.] I should like to ask you a question upon one point with regard to the Record of Title. I do not quite understand how, having it done in the way you propose, would encourage sales?
I do not think that it would encourage sales, but I think that the adoption of the other principle, that is the registering of these deeds, will lead to a great deal of confusion. One reason I have for that is, that the registration of deeds generally takes place under the name of a whole townland. In Dublin they have books in which there are indexes of these townlands. There are also indexes of the names of the parties who have purchased, or who are charged with the lands. So long as the transaction was confined to whole townlands, of course the difficulty of discovering what were the charges upon a townland was not very great, but when you have them split up into a number of small portions, and when you have these portions sold to men of probably the very same name (because in the Irish townlands you generally find a number of people of the same name on the same townland), I think you will find that a great deal of confusion will arise. Besides that, I think the expense of anything connected with further proceedings in the Registry of Deeds Office is very great, and the uncertainty is very great (if all depends upon making accurate searches), whereas if you had a sheet opened in the book, as in the case of the Record of Title, showing the owner's title to his land, and every transaction connected with it entered in that folio, one after the other, all you would have to do, in order to find out how a

man's land stood, would be to turn to that folio and see exactly what charges they were on the land.

2287. I thought I understood from you that the charges were to be bought up in the first instance?
I am assuming that these people may deal with the land afterwards by charging it in different ways. There is another point, however, and one that I consider of the greatest importance of all, in dealing with the whole of these questions of the Land Act, and it is this: I believe that the purchase clauses can never be put into universal operation, nor can there be any settlement of the agitation in Ireland with regard to the Irish land until this settlement of fair rents, as it is called, is finished. Anything that would bring about the termination of this within a given time is, I think, of the greatest possible importance. There is nothing I would impress more upon your Lordships.

2288. Chairman.] How could it ever be brought to a point? I mean how could it be ascertained when it was finished?
What I would suggest would be this: I would fix a limited time within which all applications for fixing a fair rent should be made, say a year or two years, or whatever time might be thought desirable. I should think that a year would be quite enough. Then I would say, that in any case in which an application had not been made within that time, it should be assumed that the existing rent was a fair rent, and that rent should be recognised as a fair rent, or on a statutory rent rather. I would rather call it a statutory rent than a fair rent.

2289. Lord Inchiquin.] Then you would do away with the period of 15 years, because, at present, rents are fixed for 15 years; is not that so?
No, I am speaking of putting an end to the valuation for the 15 years. We must accept the law as it is passed. Of course the statutory rent so fixed would remain for the 15 years, and only for the 15 years.

2290. Chairman.] Would not your proposal have a tendency to bring into Court many tenants, probably, that would not think much about it, and who would let things go on very much as they are now?
It would have that tendency, but I do not know that that would be any very great harm, because I believe that those tenants who are hanging back now, and not going into Court, will go in eventually, and there never will be satisfaction, I think, until the thing is settled. If they were satisfied and thought their rents were reasonable, and so on, I believe in numbers of cases they would not go in at all. The rent then would be fixed as a fair rent without any trouble and without any expense. From what I see of the working of this system, I believe it has practically resulted, and will result, in a general valuation of the whole country. I think we must accept that, and that being so, I think that valuation would be carried on much more cheaply and much more advantageously, if it were done in districts all at the same time. If there were a given time within which all the applications for fixing a fair rent were to be made, then the Land Commission would know what work they had to do in a particular district; they would know that they would have to value so many holdings, and the valuations would be made at the same time in that particular district and by the same people. I need not point out that that system would save a great deal of unnecessary expense, but I believe it would have the still further great advantage of bringing about a much more uniform settlement of rents in each district. At the present time no man can tell at what rate his rent will be fixed. The fact that a holding is valued this month by one Land Commission, is no guide or guarantee whatever to the landlord, or to the tenant either, that in six months time the holding next to it, valued by another commission, will not be valued quite differently, whereas if the valuation took place in the way I suggest (and when I call it a valuation, I may say that, I consider that the present system is a system of valuation), and were carried on over the whole of the district at once and by the same people, I consider that it would lead to much greater uniformity, and, of course, would save a great deal of expense. That then would bring about a settlement of statutory rents for

for

for 15 years, and enable both landlords and tenants to see what they could do with respect to purchasing.

2091. Lord *Brabourne.*] Has what we have had in evidence been brought to your knowledge, namely, that the farmers in England are to a great extent waiting for and expecting a new Land Bill?

I could not say that it has; I read that in Mr. Baldwin's evidence, but I think they are waiting as they say for something to turn up, they do not know exactly what.

2092. As long as there is a possibility of Parliament re-opening the question, is it likely that rents can be fixed in a permanent manner, and in such a way as to content the people?

When you speak of fixing the rent in a permanent manner, so as to content the people, I do not know that it would accomplish that, but it would enable you at once to bring about the result which is being brought about now by degrees, and it would do so in a very satisfactory way, and I believe it would lead to a general settlement of rent in a district in due time; it would also lead to more settlements between landlord and tenant than under the present arrangement.

2093. I thought your scheme was based upon the possibility of contenting the people by fixing the rent in a uniform manner?

No; my belief is that if you had this fixed rent finally settled for the 15 years that then it would be much more easy to deal with the questions of purchases and sales, and, as I said a moment ago, and as I have always held, I believe that is the ultimate settlement that must be looked forward to ere the only one that will have anything like finality about it.

2094. You mean the creation of an occupying ownership?

I do.

2095. Lord *Tyrone.*] I should like to ask you whether, in addition to the difficulty which has been raised by the noble Chairman, you do not think there would be this difficulty, that those landlords who have their properties let at a great deal below the value would be placed in a very unpleasant position by declaring that the rent was a fair rent, unless it was proved to the contrary; would not that be so?

It would be perfectly open to them, as well as to the tenants.

2096. Quite so; but look at the amount of litigation you would place upon them. If a man had a property let at a good deal below the value he might be quite satisfied to let things continue as they are now, knowing that his tenants would not bring him into Court. Rather than incur the expense and the ill-feeling occasioned by bringing his tenants into Court, might he not prefer to leave the matter as it is. If you say unless a man makes application within a year all these rents are fair, then what happens at the end of the next 15 years. Those rents will be then taken as fair rents. If he has a property let at a really fair value close by, the rents upon that property might be cut down to what be himself had admitted were fair rents, though they might be already a great deal too low?

My own impression with regard to the landlord's side of the question is, that whether he brings his tenants into Court or not, he never will be able to raise the rents again.

2097. Supposing the rents were a good deal below the value of the property, and that it was put to the landlord, either these rents must be named as fair rents or you must take your tenants all into Court, he would have the choice between those two courses?

Yes.

2098. He might not wish to go into Court, and at the same time if he did not go into Court his rents would be fixed as fair rents at a great deal below the value, would they not, according to your principle?

They would be fixed as statutory rents.

2099. Statutory rents admitted by him to be fair, because he has not gone into Court; is not that what it comes to?
Yes.

2100. That would operate in 14 years upon all the property adjoining; it would be said, "These are fair rents on this property; the rents on the property adjoining is so & so per cent. above these; therefore, we reduce the property adjoining it in the same ratio"?
I am sorry to say I do not see anything like a prospect of the settling of rents upon one property upon the ground that the rent on another property is just or fair at present.

2101. Do you consider that the rents, in the way they are now being fixed, are very unequal?
I do; I consider that they are very unequal. On the vast bulk of my property I have what I consider to be very low rents, and I know that I, as an individual, should be delighted to get them, without any trouble, agreed to by the tenants, and recorded as fair rents; but my apprehension is that if I were to go into Court to have these existing low rents recorded, they would be reduced, low as they are, because I believe the general tendency is to reduce. I know that I should most gladly accept from any tenant the recording of the lowest rent upon my estate for the 15 years if he would agree to accept it.

2102. Then you have no belief in the fairness of the Courts?
I do not wish to find fault with the constitution of the Courts; but I am bound to say that I have no faith in the principle of the whole system.

2103. Lord Brabourne.] Have you been able to discover a principle, because that is what we have been trying to do?
I think it is the absence of principle that is the difficulty. I held before the Land Act was ever passed, and I will hold, that this result must take place. You cannot expect that rents could be really fixed at the full or fair value by persons going down in the way they do under the present system, knowing very little about the circumstances of any particular holding. It must be more or less a guess.

The Witness is directed to withdraw.

Ordered, That this Committee be adjourned sine die.

APPENDIX.

LIST OF APPENDIX.

APPENDIX.

Appendix A.

PAPERS handed in by Mr. *G. H. Smith*, 1 June 1883.

(A.)

Decision pronounced by Mr. Sub-Commissioners *Wylie* (Barrister-at-Law), *Smith*, and *Ferguson*, at *Portadown*, 27th April 1883, in Cases of *W. Williamson* (Tenant), *F. R. Gage*, Esq. (Landlord), heard at *Armagh*, April 1883 (copied from Report in "Northern Whig" of 30th April 1883, which was printed from MS. of Mr. *Wylie*, Barrister-at-Law).

" In these cases of Williamson's, I regret to have to state that my colleagues have reported to me a circumstance which, I am glad to say, is of very rare occurrence in this or any other county I have had experience of. The tenant, at the hearing, proved a very large number of acres of thorough drainage, and my colleagues, when testing the evidence on inspection, discovered that, at the ordinary intervals for thorough drainage, a number of false mouths had been made to indicate the existence of drains. But when these were cleared out it was seen that no drain whatever existed there. Being unable, in consequence of this, to place any reliance on the tenant's evidence, we have only allowed for such improvements as were plainly visible on inspection."

(B.)

Tabular Analysis of the Judicial Rents fixed in above Cases, after the delivery of above Judicial Observations.

Tenant's Name.	1. Old Rent.	2. Valuation of Mr. Kenyon, for Tenant.	3. Valuation of Mr. McBryde, for Landlord.	4. Total of Columns 2 and 3.	5. Mean of Amount in Column 4.	6. Judicial Rent.
	£. s. d.	£. s. d.	£. s. d.	£. s. d.	£. s. d.	£. s. d.
	20 0 0	19 3 -	18 4 3	34 7 8	17 3 9	17 - -
	14 - -	18 4 -	19 16 -	37 10 -	18 16 8	18 9 -
	20 - -	20 - -	20 16 -	44 16 -	24 8 -	24 - -
W. Williamson	10 - -	9 4 -	10 1 8	19 4 4	9 3 9	9 - -
	4 10 -	6 - -	1 9 -	7 4 -	9 11 4	6 12 6
	42 17 -	41 - 6	45 3 10	89 9 1	44 1 8	19 15 -
£.	120 10 0	104 19 0	120 1 5	204 11 3	118 7 1	140 12 6

Being a difference on the six holdings between the "agricultural" and "judicial" prices (in favour of tenant, whose evidence was judicially discredited) of 8 14 7

£ 118 7 1

(C.)

Abstract of Decisions pronounced at Castlereagh, 21st May 1883, by Mr. Sub Commissioner Foley, &c., in Cases on Estate of F. P. Garrette, Esq., heard at Cloghan, May 1883 (by Messrs. Kirk and Byers, sitting (by consent) alone during Absence of the Legal Sub-Commissioner in London.

TENANTS.	1. Old Rent.	2. Valuation given for Tenant.	3. Valuation given for Landlord.	4. Total of Columns 2 and 3.	5. Moiety of Amount in Column 4.	6. Judicial Rent.
	£. s. d.	£. s. d.	£. s. d.	£. s. d.	£. s. d.	£. s. d.
Hackett						
O'Hagan						
Nixon						
M'Loughlin						
Wilson						
D. Nunn						
M'Mullen						
Bradley						
R. Daly						
Bradley (2)						
M'Sorley						
Hacket (2)						
M'Keown						
Campbell						

Being a difference in seven cases between the "arithmetical" and "judicial" amounts of only

(D.)

Tabular Analysis of Decisions pronounced 29th May 1883, at Armagh, of Cases on Estate of Rev. Walter Riddell, heard at Armagh, 23rd May 1883, by Messrs. Wylie (Barrister-at-Law), Smith, and Ferguson.

TENANT.	1. Old Rent.	2. Valuation given for Tenant.	3. Valuation given for Landlord.	4. Total of Columns 2 and 3.	5. Moiety of Amount in Column 4.	6. Judicial Rent.
	£. s. d.	£. s. d.	£. s. d.	£. s. d.	£. s. d.	£. s. d.
F. Mallon						
R. M'Callaghan						
A. M'Caskey						
J. Flanagan						
J. Webb						
R. Hughes						
P. Mallon						

Being a difference in seven cases between "arithmetical" and "judicial" process of only

(E.)

TABULAR ANALYSIS of Decisions pronounced at Coolattin, 29th May 1882, on Cases on Estate of Chas. G. B. Kennedy, Esq., heard at Coolattin, 15th May 1882, by Messrs. Foley, (Q.C.), Montgomery, and Simpson.

Tenants.	1. Old Rent.	2. Valuation given for Tenant.	3. Valuation given for Landlord.	4. Total of Columns 2 and 3.	5. Meity of Amount in Column 4.	6. Judicial Rent.
	£. s. d.	£. s. d.	£. s. d.	£. s. d.	£. s. d.	£. s. d.
R. Wilson	26 5 6	20 18 0	27 11 2	48 9 4	24 1 8	25 - -
R. M'Kernan	22 7 6	16 10 7	21 2 1	38 10 4	18 7 10	17 10 -
J. Miller	20 9 3	17 7 -	20 10 9	37 17 9	18 18 10	17 - -
J. Stewart	8 5 -	6 - 9	6 6 11	11 5 8	5 13 10	5 - -
Jas. Miller	22 17 -	17 19 6	34 6 5	55 6 10	31 1 11	30 10 -
J. Bennett	11 16 -	9 18 -	10 16 1	19 19 1	9 16 6½	8 5 -
J. Lockhart	21 18 9	15 9 10	19 10 -	35 0 10	17 10 5	17 10 -
R. Shepherd	34 7 8	26 19 5	31 19 5	57 19 10	28 19 5	27 10 -
£.	164 17 5	131 18 5	171 3 9	290 6 -	154 13 9	149 5 -

Being a difference on eight cases between " arithmetical " and } " judicial " proven of 5 7 9

£. 154 13 9

* In these two cases the judicial rent is fixed under the amount of the tenants' own valuation.

(F.)

COPY of CIRCULAR issued by the Irish Land Commission Court since the delivery of the Judgment of Common Pleas Divisional Court, Dublin, in Glenn v. Nolan.

DATE OF COMMENCEMENT OF JUDICIAL RENT.

The view of the Irish Land Commissioners on this subject has been that when an application, grounded on the tenant's originating notice to fix a fair rent, was served in court on the first occasion of the sitting of the Court, and stood adjourned, the case came within the provisions of the Land Law Act, and that the order made thereon, fixing the fair rent, had the same effect as if it had been made on the day on which that first application was made. And consequently, on this construction of the statute the judicial rent would begin to accrue due, in such a case, from the gale-day next succeeding the passing of the Act (22nd August 1881). The Common Pleas Divisional of the High Court of Justice has, however, now decided that the same matters has not the effect above-mentioned, and that the judicial rent in every case begins to accrue due from the gale-day next after the second decision fixing such rent, and not earlier.

21 May 1882.

Denis Godley.

(G.)

Copy of APPEAL LIST as used by Court at Omagh, on 16th May 1843.

COURT VALUER'S REPORTS.—COURT OF THE LAND COMMISSION.

Appeals from Sub-Commissioners and County Courts fixed for hearing at Omagh on Wednesday, the 16th day of May 1843. (Adjourned from Sittings at Omagh and Strabane.)

Also to be heard by Special Order the Undermentioned Applications in the Case of Michael Quinn and James Ball, Tenants; and J. M. Savage, Landlord.

APPEALS.—Court Tenures.

List No.	Appeal No.	Record No.	Tenant.	Landlord.	Appellant	Observations. Court Valuer's Report.
						£. s. d.
1	97	194	William Denney	John Denley and William Denley.	L.	Adjourned.
2	8.9	391	Terence M'Cusker	Charles Denley, m.p.	L.	8 10 –
3	9.9	619	John Campbell	......	L.	24 12 9
4	864	623	Edward M'Nally	......	L.	9 – –
5	7.44	623	Owen M'Cusker	......	L.	12 6 –
6	9.58	629	John M'Gedrick	......	L.	6 5 –
7	109	County Court.	Bridget M'Cullagh	Robert William Lowry	L.	}
8	110	County Court.	Patrick M'Cullagh	......	L.	}
9	111	County Court.	Philip Donnelly	......	L.	} Withdrawn.
10	112	County Court.	Archibald Johnston	......	L.	}
11	114	County Court.	Representatives of Felix Donnelly.	......	L.	}
12	116	563	Margaret Dale	F. J. Gervais	T.	85 10 –
13	117	569	James Mulligan	......	T.	17 – –
14	198	827	Joseph M'Laughlin	S. Yates Johnston	L.	14 16 –
15	199	663	George Swith	......	L.	87 – –
16	209	694	William Irvine	......	L.	19 – –
17	991	695	Lanty Gormley	......	L.	90 10
18	971	696	Thomas M'Crede	......	L.	93 4 –
19	999	710	John M'Crede	......	L.	11 5 –
20	901	711	Patrick Kane	......	L.	85 10 –
21	809	715	James Gallagher	......	L.	6 15 –
22	999	719	Thomas Irvine	......	L.	40 – –
23	9.9	75	John Rutledge	Mervyn Archdale	L.	17 – –
24	961	476	James M'Brien	Colonel J. G. Irvine	T.	99 16 –
25	849		......	......	L.	}
26	999	477	Edward Breen	......	T.	17 1 –
27	849		......	......	L.	}

APPEALS—COUNTY TYRONE—continued.

List No.	Appeal No.	Record No.	Tenant.	Landlord.	Appellant.	Observations. Court Valuer's Report.
						£ s. d.
78 79	889 341	688	Robert Neville	Colonel J. G. Irvine	T. L.	14 14 —
30 31	844 345	691	Richard Wilson	ditto	T. L.	30 — —
32 33	245 244	601	William Cliff	ditto	T. L.	30 — —
34 35	687 728	603	John M'Quaid	ditto	T. L.	19 — —
36 37	287 240	699	Charles M'Dade	ditto	T. L.	14 14 —
38 39	708 244	675	William M'Aleer	ditto	T. L.	15 5 —
40	132	County Court.	Jos. Wiley, jun.	Rev B. Blacker	L.	20 10 —
41	870	687	James Clarke	Sir Wm. E. H. Verner	L.	27 10 —
42 43	369 776	617	Thomas M'Caughey	Captain James Surrey	T. L.	7 16 —
44 45	670 778	380	Charles Chittick	ditto	T. L.	12 10 —
46 47	671 677	318	Michael M'Caughey	ditto	T. L.	21 5 —
48 49	872 778	618	Christopher Carr	ditto	T. L.	16 — —
50	873	464	Thomas Teague	James Surry	L.	Withdrawn.
51	274	809	Charles M'Aleer	ditto	L.	
52	889	636	Francis Kequrn	Robert Bleakley	T.	6 6 —
53	168	2,184	James Simms	Duke of Abercorn	L.	12 10 — (Dismissed.)
54	170	2,484	Robert Wilson	ditto	L.	25 — —
55	164	2,185	James Slevins	Representatives of James Rankin.	L.	27 10 — (Stands for judgment.)
56	180	171	Michael M'Cullagh	James Humphreys	L.	5 5 —
57	194	170	Patrick M'Cullagh	ditto	L.	6 — —
58	185	607	Catherine Conway	James M'Partland	L.	6 — —

(M.)

LAND COMMISSION COURT—Appeal Sittings in Omagh, 16 May 1882.

ANALYSIS of Cases decided on the Appeals.

	Old Rent.	Sub-Commissioners' Rent.	Court Valuer's Estimate.	Appeal Rent.
	£ s. d.	£ s. d.	£ s. d.	£ s. d.
Estate of Charles Demsley, M. D.:				
No. 2 on Appeal List	11 - -	7 10 -	8 10 -	7 10 -
No. 3 „ „ „	23 8 4	15 -	24 15 9	13 - -
No. 4 „ „ „	10 10 -	6 10 -	9 - -	6 10 -
No. 5 „ „ „	12 10 -	10 10 -	12 5 -	10 10 -
No. 6 „ „ „	7 -	3 10 -	3 5 -	3 10 -
	£ 43 - -	60 15 9	40 - -

4 Rents confirmed on appeal.

1 Rent raised on appeal.

(Entire rents, by appeal decisions, left 14 l. 15 s. 9 d. under Court Valuer's estimate.)

Estate of F. P. Gervais:—		£ s. d.
Nos. 12 and 13 on List	Sub-Commissioners' rents	40 - -
	Appeal decisions	40 - -
	Court Valuer's estimate	43 10 -

Estate of S. Yates Johnstone :—		
Nos. 14 to 23 on List	Sub-Commissioners' rents	159 10 -
	Appeal decisions	165 10 -
	Court Valuer's estimate	195 - -

(Final decisions, 29 l. 10 s. less than Court Valuer's estimate.)

Estate of Colonel Irvine :—		
8 Cases on List	Sub-Commissioners' rents	116 - -
	Appeal decisions	123 10 -
	Court Valuer's estimate	141 16 -

(Final decisions, 38 l. 6 s. less than Court Valuer's estimate.)

Estate of Captain Storey :		
4 Cases on List	Sub-Commissioners' rents	37 10 -
	Appeal rents	37 10 -
	Court Valuer's estimate	46 5 -

(Final decisions, 18 l. 15 s. less (or 23 per cent. less) than Court Valuer's estimate.)

(Other cases on list settled, adjourned for judgment on law points, or dismissed.)

SUMMARY of 26 Cases.

	£ s. d.
Judicial rents fixed by Sub-Commissioners -	398 - -
Made as result of appeals -	418 10 -
In cases where the Court Valuer's estimate of value (in several of them as "leaving a substantial interest to the tenant") was -	516 5 9

That is to say, besides leaving the tenants a substantial interest in their holdings, the Court has deducted from their own Court Valuer's estimate of a fair rent for "improvements" (already taken into account in the "substantial interest" of each tenant) about 20 per cent.

APPENDIX B.

PAPERS handed in by Mr. *W. H. Gray*, 1 June 1883.

JUDICIAL RENTS as fixed by Sub-Commissioners at *Kells*, County Meath, 7th July 1882.

ESTATE of Rev. *C. B. Scott*, D.D.

TENANTS' NAME.	Old Rent.	When Fixed.	Poor Law Valuation.	Valuations.			New Rent.	Tenant's Interest.
				Tenants' Value.	Landlords' Value.	Mean of Value.		
	£. s. d.		£. s. d.	£. s. d.	£. s. d.	£. s. d.	£. s. d.	£. s. d.
James Tuohy * - - - -	35 10 0	1844 -	35 10 –	31 7 –	45 4 11	37 16 0	35 – –	315 – –
William Mackin - - -	80 – –	1841 - -	40 10 –	49 – –	61 17 10	49 18 –	46 10 –	700 – –
James Mulvany - - - -	173 14 0	Part 1814, part 1846.	165 15 –	174 15 –	179 2 5	148 10 10	161 5 –	535 16 –
John Mulvany - - - -	47 9 1	1830 - -	37 – –	34 0 0	40 19 7	43 14 1	40 – –	450 – –
Anne Carroll † - - - -	150 0 –	1860 - -	84 – –	99 12 –	‡ 100 16 0	‡ 110 14 10	110 – –	Interest not fixed.
£. - - -	464 0 0	- - -	434 16 –	393 8 0	459 2 0	[illegible] 8 0	[illegible] 15 –	–

* £. 1. 0 s. added to rent in 1873, for an expenditure on buildings by the landlord of 15 l.
† £. 10. 0 s. added to rent in 1873, for an expenditure on building a new house of 200 l.
‡ Value of house built by landlord excluded.

SALES of FARM TENANCIES, under the Irish Land Act, 1881. (Compiled for and published with "Farmers' Gazette." of Saturday, 2nd June 1883.)

SUMMARY.

SMALL REDUCTIONS.

Tenant.	Landlord.	Old Rent.	Mr. Gray's Valuation.	Judicial Rent.
		£. s. d.	£. s. d.	£. s. d.
James Dillon -	- Mrs. A. H. Canfield	1 16 6	1 10 -	1 6 -
Thos. Neales -	- ditto - -	16 10 6	16 10 -	17 10 -
Michael Carroll -	Lord Longford -	80 16 9	80 10 -	84 - -
John Walsh -	- ditto - -	98 - -	93 6 -	88 - -
Pat. Casey -	Lady Ashtown -	11 10 -	11 - -	10 - -
Mary O'Connor -	ditto - -	10 - -	8 17 6	8 - -

PAPER put in by the Irish Land Commissioners.

The Irish Land Commission,
34, Upper Merrion-street, Dublin,
15 June 1882.

Sir,

I am directed by the Irish Land Commissioners to send, for the information of the Committee of the House of Lords, the enclosed return of sales effected under Part V. of the Land Law Act.

It is not known whether the rents stated are judicial rents or not, nor can the tenure be stated without much further delay, inasmuch as where the lands for sale are free-farm, but are sold indemnified against rent by other lands, the tenure has been incorrectly described in many of the applications for loans, and it would be necessary to refer in every case to the solicitor.

Where the lands have been sold subject to fee-farm grants, the outgoings are stated in Column (N.)

The Commissioners are not always aware whether the balance of purchase money is paid in cash or secured by mortgage, inasmuch as the terms stated in the original applications are sometimes changed before completion.

Column (F.) shews under what section the advances have been made.

Loans under Section 14 are in case of sales between landlord and tenant by agreement.

Loans under Section 26, where the estate has been bought by the Land Commission for re-sale to the tenants.

Loans under Section 35, where the tenant has purchased in the Land Judges' Court.

A schedule of pending and abandoned cases would take a very long time to prepare, and it is thought that it will be more convenient to their Lordships that this return should be sent forward at once.

I am, &c.
(signed)   Denis Godley.

The Hon. E. Thesiger.

IRISH LAND COMMISSION.—SALES TO TENANTS.

RETURN of Advances under Part V., ss. 24, 26, 25, from 22nd August 1881 up to 22nd May 1882.

COUNTY ANTRIM:

COUNTY ARMAGH—*Nil.*

COUNTY CARLOW:

COUNTY CAVAN:

COUNTY CLARE—*Nil.*

COUNTY CORK:

COUNTY DONEGAL—*Nil.*

FOURTH

REPORT

FROM THE

SELECT COMMITTEE OF THE HOUSE OF LORDS

ON

LAND LAW (IRELAND);

TOGETHER WITH THE

PROCEEDINGS OF THE COMMITTEE

MINUTES OF EVIDENCE,

AND APPENDIX.

Ordered, by The House of Commons, to be Printed,
27 July 1883.

[*Price 8½ d.*]

279.

Under 6 oz.

INDEX.

INDEX TO REPORT.

ANALYSIS OF INDEX.

LIST of the PRINCIPAL HEADINGS in the following INDEX, with the Pages at which they may be found.

INDEX TO MINUTES OF EVIDENCE.

[Note.—Questions 1 to 1627 appear in the Third Report; 1628 to 2103 in the Fourth Report.)

Baldwin, Mr. Thomas. [Analysis of his Evidence]—continued.

Judicial Rents, Future of (1370, 1371, 1373, 1374, 1416-1417, 1421-1427, 1440, 1443-1447)——And when tenant-right has been purchased (1387-1390, 1411, 2012, 2144)——In cases of cheap sales (2283-1292, 2303, 2341, 1292-1296)——Difference of decisions of Sub-Commissioners in such cases (1331, 1332)——Where assistance not obtained (1043-1045).

Reduction of Rent (1368, 1369)——Average of, made (1242-1243)——Effect on landlords of (1246-1253, 1403); made no abatement of ....

(1.) Sir R. Wallace (1285-1270, 1367, 1392, 1393).

(2.) Lord Lurgan, Lord Gosford, Duke of Manchester (1872-1875).

(3.) Colonel King-Harman (1342-1347).

Land Act, Working of (1010-1042, 1043-1091, 1073-1074, 2280, 2281, 1385, 1410-1430, 1432, 1437-1440).

Purchase Clauses of, working of (1684, 1685-1688, 1491, 1493, 1530, 1531)——Few purchases under tatler (1484)——But tenant often willing to purchase (1438, 1490, 1491-1494)——and landlord to sell holding (1498-1500).

Money borrowed from State likely to be repaid (1502, 1503).

Present proprietors life would be benefited (1485-1497, 1505).

Drainage, working of Land Act in regard to (1457-1458).

Reclamation, working of Land Act in regard to, unsatisfactory (1450, 1451)——and Government schemes for, unattainable (1451).

Administration of, cost of (1235-1240, 1393)——Greater than that of Griffith's valuation (1396, 1397, 1432-1439).

Land, opinion as to valuation of (1908-1010, 1070, 1071, 1443).

Depreciation of, difficulty in questions of (1081-1087).

Value of, in proximity to towns (1430, 1431)——Candidate at present (1430)——but should be made saleable by the State (1056)——Such action would be beneficial (1057).

Rent as, in Ireland generally low (1436, 1436)——and good investments of money impossible (1434, 1421-1474, 1476-1479).

Landlords, losses incurred by, under Land Act (1497)——Especially when land purchased in Encumbered Estates Court (1410).

Sub-Commissioners, inspection of Land by (1126-1128, 1294, 6911-1815)——Buildings seldom visited by legal members, but under penalties not included (1126-1131)——Power to fix rent by Sub-Commissioners (1213-1217)——increase of Rents (1021-1096)——particulars of improvements not being given (1096).

Assignments, difficulty of dealing with questions of (1080, 1081)——No official record kept of when made with (1081, 1082)——Rent should not default to paying (1082)——and should be made (1081-1090)——Possibility of tenant claiming after fifteen years for, now allowed for (1379-1381).

Legal Questions to be decided by Legal Sub-Commissioner (1134-1137, 1142, 1144, 1145, 1325, 1326).

Value of land and improvements, questions of, to be decided by Lay Sub-Commissioner (1142).

Rent, fixture of, virtually fixed by Lay Sub-Commissioners (1143, 1327, 1338).

Appeal Court, procedure and examination of (1418-1420, 1321, 1324)——Evidence before, previous to hearing of case (1214-1231).

Official Valuers of, number and duties of (1129-1228)——Influence of reports of valuers on Appeal Court (1329-1331, 1322, 1329).

Valuers, Professional, valuations of, equally trustworthy and to be allowed (1211)——but expense of, often incalculable (1177-1211, 1325, 1293-1325)——Valuation apparently used in deciding valuations (1181-1198, 1199-1226, 1212).

Migration and Emigration of Tenants, necessary (1458-1464, 1446, 1459, 1624, 1626, 3216, 1321-1325, 1325)——and should take place before purchase of holdings (1311-1316)——Emigration, working of Land Act as regards (2336, 1479, 1480).

Small Holdings, number of, not decreased (1465-1466, 2418)——but subdivision should be prevented (1517-1520)——and tendency to sub-division has increased (1519).

Deterioration of Land, under tenant (1480).

Removal of Tenant, compensation to be made for (1490-1492).

Map, or plan of holdings, ought to be produced (1080-1089, 1101, 1105-1107, 1126-1128)——as Sub-Commissioners have been to rely on statement of tenant (1130). Necessary as Official Valuers, but not namely produced (1101, 1106, 1111, 1121).

Accuracy

Third and Fourth Reports, 1833—continued.

Baldwin, Mr. Thomas. (Analysis of his Evidence)—continued.

Accuracy as to land sales disputes without, difficult (1100, 1104)——Particularly necessary, when Rundale System prevails (1109-1113, 1116-1119).

Rundale System, Land Commissioners should have power to re-arrange property now under (1839-1841).

Re-distribution of Holdings, would be popular (1525-1528)——and beneficial (1529-1533, 1525).

Cost of Government, in Ireland, has increased (1508, 1509).

Adams v. Denscroth, effect of decision in (1033, 1825, 1578-1581).

Bell v. Rabinson, case of (Smith 460).

Blake v. Lord Clarina, case of (Wright 1611).

Brady, Sir F., decision of (Smith 480).

C.

Cases, frequent adjournments of, owing to inexperience etc. of Land Commission, Chief Witness (10, 11)——Delay of, before Sub-Commissioners (Chambers 1807-1810)——An arrangement of, to be desirable, by Sub-Commissioners (Baldwin 112, 113)——Number of greater, able to be decided in County Courts (Barker 306)——Settlements of, out of court (Smith 337-339; Baldwin 117, 118, 119, 1116; Chambers 1759-1768, 1788, 1787)——Detailing, prolonged (Chambers 211, 212; Foley 698-701, 703, 704, 821, 834-834)——Evidence on in, before Appeals Court (Baldwin 1316-1325)——History of, not given to official witness (Wright 1663).

Chains v. Nixon, case of (Smith 1648).

Champion, Mr. Hunt. (Analysis of his Evidence)——An examination and land agent (1836)——Sub-Commissioners, changes of, frequent and injurious (1783-1786, 1780)——Changes of, approving present fix (1798, 1799).

Cost, delay of, before Sub-Commission, Court, and consequent, expense to suitors (1607, 1638)——Such delay might be obviated (1649-1646)——Full Commissioners apparently unwilling to avoid expense or harrying suits (1665-1679)——No official report of particulars of official cases, kept by (1671)——Return of, now thereby necessary (1673-1674)——Such reports might be easily kept (1676, 1677).

Inspection of Holdings, by (1684-1696, 1787-1790).

Decision of, and Nature of Rent, by, easy, and consequent difficulty of settlement out of court (1701-1709, 1285, 1787).

Principle of Decisions of, difficult to describe (1735, 1784)——Rules put by, as—

(i.) Holdings over yearns (1781).

(ii.) Accommodation holdings (1722, 1723).

Tenant-right, Tenant fix, made, by Sub-Commissioners (1765)——Tenant-right sold for high price, although rents have been reduced (1812-1824).

Value, Capital in, not given by Sub-Commissioners (1878, 1879)——and uncertainty difficulty as to appeals (1880).

Land unsaleable, at present (1894)——Different Land, rent fixed on, unduly (1891-1681)——Deteriorate Land, fixture of rent on, unsatisfactory (1887-1890).

Rent reduced, although valuations made a short time previously (1644, 1681).

Valuations for Tenant, often unreliable (1726, 1727).

Improvements of Tenant, evidence as to unreliable (1888)——Tenant not held in particulars of improvements given (Foley 1895)——Statement of Improvements claimed should be given by complaining notice (1889)——Possible claim by tenant after fifteen years for improvements already allowed for (1678, 1782)——Questions of, claimed, difficult to decide (1737, 1783).

(i.) Drainage (1708-1711, 1714-1718, 1736, 1745)——Made by tenant often various (1718, 1744, 1747)——but allowed for in improvements (1745, 1746)——Deduction for, made often before given (1740, 1741)——Tenant not compelled to keep drains in repair (1747-1750, 1720)——Consequent deterioration of land, need not in other respects (1751-1754).

(ii.) Fences, made often injurious (1755, 1744)——But allowed for as improvements (1751, 1753, 1754)——Claim made for, greater than rent paid (1746, 1752).

(iii.) Reclamation, claims for extravagant (1738-1740, 1788)——Reclamation made for (176)-1766, 1770, 1771, 1774)——Howards made for (1765, 1757, 1758)——in other injurious (1763, 1766——" Caprices" for (1765, 1771-1782)——Value of land reclaimed (1772, 1774).

(125—Page)   14   (iv.) Buildings,

Third and Fourth Reports, 1883—continued.

Chambers, Mr. Hurt. [Analysis of his Evidence]—continued.

(iv.) Rankings, allowance for, made to landlord (1764).

Valuations, weight of, as to estimate of Land Commissioners (1548-1551, 1756-1811, 1814-1816).

Value, a division as to, of Baths weighed with Sub-Commissioners (1729-1732).

Chalmers, John, case of (Smith 636).

Compensation, cannot be obtained by tenant for both improvements and rights, under their contract (Before 561)—Holmes, given for their rights than for improvements (Holmes 87).

Costs, Rules of Land Commissioners as regards, in Appeals (Holmes 90-98).
   (i.) Of application to Chief Commissioners (Smith 351, 365-369).
   (ii.) To arrange, of ordinary notice as to particulars of improvements (Smith 347, 348).
   (iii.) Of complying with original order to furnish such particulars (Smith 349-351).
   (iv.) Of voids, in landlord, not Landlord.

Counsel, exception of improvements out of Land Commission Court (Holmes 9)—cannot do, improvements of rights from allowance of, working up improvements out (Holmes 10, 11).
   Unable to decide proper state of law as regards Level (Holmes 83).
   Unable to decide on which principle Land Commissioners act (Holmes 115, 117, 118).
   Inapplicance of, by landlords (1357, 1358).

County Court, unsatisfactory working of Land Act, 1881, before (Reeve 595, 596 ; Baldwin 1189-1195)—Working of, under Land Act, 1870 (Wright 1573).
   Appeals under Civil Bill Act, resort to (Wright 1633).

D.

Decision of Court of Appeal (Holmes 115-119 ; Smith 408, 414).
   Of Chief Commissioners (Holmes 96, 105 ; Smith 441-458)—as regards date from which judicial rent due (Smith 1948).
   Of Sub-Commissioners (Holmes 23, 24, 33, 42, 98, 114 ; Reeve 300, 306, 222, 323, 391-394, 398-392, 394, 595, 599-300, 304-308, 319, 330 ; Smith 422-427, 484, 479, 515, 516 ; Fairy 683, 794 ; Baldwin 1021, 1027, 1313, 1415 ; Wright 1558 ; Chambre 1701-1705, 1763, 1787).
   No uniformity in, of Sub-Commissioners (Holmes 42 ; Smith 425-427 ; Fairy 784, 786 ; Baldwin 1031-1033, 1147, 1145, 1307-1310).
   Difference of, in different members of Sub-Commission (Holmes 33-36).
   Character of, affected by changes in composition of Sub-Commission (Holmes 123).
   Reasons for required (Reeve 315, 316 ; Smith 493-461 ; Fairy 679-701, 721-930, 832-943, 1000 ; Baldwin 1372-1374 ; Wright 1554-1557, 1560, 1596-1569, 1637).
   Principle of (Holmes 111 ; Smith 554-557, 409-431, 443-446, 443-454 ; Fairy 787, 804, 815, 816 ; Baldwin 1006, 1007, 1045-1030, 1048, 1105, 1313, 1345-1364 ; Wright 1564-1568, 1577-1570, 1589-1588, 1604 ; Chambre 1783, 1734 ; Grey 1635, 1641, 1645-1680, 1672-1678, 1691-1697 ; O'Conor Don 2105, 2103).
   Instructions as to principle of (Holmes 47-53 ; Fairy 999, 1000 ; Baldwin 1013, 1014, 1018-1020, 1039, 1031-1034, 1045-1068, 1074-1077, 1159-1164, 1416, 1421, 1422)—Results of no instructions as to, being given (Baldwin 1021-1030).
   As to Drainage difficult (Grey 1620-1623, 1637, 1947, 1946, 1850, 1851, 2011-2012).
   Apparently given in favour of tenant (Smith 349).
   Adams v. Dunsmith, in case of. See Adams v. Dunsmith.
   Mr. Justice O'Hagan, of. See O'Hagan.
   Sir F. Brady, of. See Brady.

E.

Emigration of Tenant. See Tenant.
   Working of Land Act as regards. See Land Law (Ireland) Act, 1881.
Encumbrancer. See Mortgagee.

Ennis,

Third and Fourth Reports, 1880—continued.

F.

Faby, Mr. Ramsay. (Analysis of his Evidence.)—A legal Sub-Commissioner (656)—An owner of land (657), but has had no practical experience in management of landed property (677, 719, 721, 925)—Has had rents reduced on property, but has not appealed (991).

Sub-Commission, procedure of (680, 625, 696, 677–691).

Sub-Commissioners, tenure of office by (656)—Transfers of, made apparently on no fixed principle (650)—Are not considered as to being removed (467)—Reason for removal of (650–671)—Present arrangement of (944, 945)—Arrangement of, left to legal member (719–820, 656–964).

Questions of value decided by Lay Sub-Commissioners, but in cases of great discrepancy, or of difference of opinion between lay members, legal member intervenes (676–678, 719–721, 722–725, 794–797, 811, 855–856, 993, 998).

Legal Sub-Commissioner, legal questions decided by (675, 840, 842–851, 1969–96)—Interference of, in questions of value, difficult (722, 836, 866)—And questions of value difficult to decide (737–739).

Sub-Commissioners, Proceedings of, Evidence of, under other Sub-Commissioners not to be accepted (752–754)—Want of uniformity in decisions likely to result (755, 754).

Principles of decision, Instructions as to, not given to Sub-Commissioners (757, 779).

Reasons for decision, required from Sub-Commissioners, but not given (926–930, 933–943, 1000).

Value as estimated by Sub-Commissioners (737–745).

Valuation of holdings by Sub-Commissioners (752–797, 801, 819, 840–865——Principle as to, uncertain (801–802, 818–819).

Original Rent left unaltered, and in some cases raised (767–771).

Inspection of Holdings by Sub-Commissioners (789–791, 879, 821).

Improvements allowed for, by Sub-Commissioners (802, 815–816, 853–856, 864–872, 884, 893–917).

Produce, alterations in price of, considered by Sub-Commissioners (874–876).

Official Valuers, Reports of, rules of Sub-Commissioners as regards (835–840, 842, 843).

Mortgages, rules of Sub-Commissioners as regards (869–876).

Land, selling value of, opinion of Mr. Justice O'Hagan as regards (746–749)—Sales of, seldom occur (658).

Encumbrancers unable to obtain money from encumbered estates (659–661)—But do not usually endeavour to enforce payment from owners (662).

Depreciation of, considered by Sub-Commissioners (806–811).

Evidence as to value of, given by tenant, and not given by landlord (675)——Evidence given to be accepted, if no opposing evidence given (675, 658)——But no rule

(136—Ind.)   **K**

Foley, Mr. Romney. (Analysis of his Evidence)—continued.

made as that effect (691, 694)——Difference of opinion of Sub-Commissioners with regard to such additions being taken (671)——Acts appeal to Appeal Court, causing these taken (691–692).

Holding being illegally sub-improved by Sub-Commissioners (687);

Evidence on behalf of landlord often not given, valuations of Sub-Commissioners being relied on (805);

Middlemen, no notice given to landlord, when concerned (774–775);

Improvements, Notice of, ought to be given by tenant to landlord (863–864).

Improvements, questions as to, made by tenant, etc. etc. (668)——Where equity unable to specify improvements, and considers temporarily all improvement, so required reduction of rent, not ought to be continued (693, 700)——Although such decision often required (701).

Rent, fixing of, by Sub-Commissioners (822–824; 913–937, 967, 988, 983–994)——Small reductions of, ought not to be made (942–953).

Judicial, confirmed on appeal (829, 832).

Tenant right, value of, with occupancy had large sums of money given for (863–864)——Questions of, difficult to decide (758–759, 812–860, 891–896, 897).

Value of, difficult to decide (757–761)——Considered by Sub-Commissioners in deciding questions of value, but to what extent uncertain (863, 769)——Rent not to be reduced solely on account of (712–743)——Value of improvements and tenant-right should differ (718–743).

Sale of, pending service (918–920).

Purchase of, what repaid, a proof of largeness of rent (920, 923).

Value of Holding, payment of rent for number of years no best criterion of (796, 798–779, 801)——Even though high price paid for tenant-right (792)——As history of rent should be considered (793, 791, 883);

Cost, questions as to history of, often asked, but ought not to be answered (826–831).

Valuers, professional, not employed by Tenant, but neighbouring farmers taken (who wish a rent to be decided) value for each other (874, 878, 884)——Such valuations unreliable (887–888)——Act for landlord, not make reductions in rent (874).

Forest v. Nixon, case of (Judge 1602).

Rent, as to improvements, to be filled in, by Sub-Commissioners (859, p. 189) (Rooms 201, 205, 216; rooms 371, 375, 376–383, 386, 389, 391, 392; Appendix 1041, 1045, 1513–1517)——Rather filled in by official valuers. See Valuer.

Fair Court, Memoir of, from Land Commission Court (Holmes 8, 9).

G.

Godley, Mr., letter from, to Sub-Commissioners with regard to giving reasons for decisions (Foley 949).

Gray, Mr. W. P. (Analysis of his Evidence)—A farmer and magistrate (1861–1866)——Has acted as official valuer (1367–1371, 1672–1683).

Improvement of, reasons for (1384–1388, 1898–1904).

Rents, principle on which fixed (1678–1876).

Sub-Commission, procedure of (1881, 1882).

Sub-Commissioners, appointment of, for limited period unsatisfactory (1889–1903).

Proceedings of, difference in (1849–1903)——Lack of principle on which they act (1881–1897).

Reductions of Holdings by, rapid, and likely to produce mistakes (1851–1855, 1882)——Explanation made by asking too (1856, 1901)——Parties interested not always present (1925–1931, 1932).

Rent, fixing of, by one Sub-Commissioner and values (1887)——Small reductions of, condemn (p. 44) (1888)——Reductions of, large increased (1900, 1901).

Valuation of Sub-Commissioners and official values, compared (1841, 1848–1858).

Valuers, instructions given to, as to procedure, but not of principle of valuation (1868, 1891, 1893–1897).

Inspection of Holdings by (1918–1922, 1895, 1896, 2028, 2029, 2028–2027, 2036, 2046, 2048–2057).

Third and Fourth Reports, 1845—continued.

Gray, Mr. W. H. (Analysis of his Evidence—continued).

Form to be filled up by (...)

Maps seldom furnished, but are necessary (...)

...

H.

High Court of Justice (Probate, &c. Division), removal of, to **Four Courts (Holmes)**

...

Holmes, Mr. H., Q.C. (Analysis of his Evidence)—Has been Solicitor General for Ireland (...)

...

(i.) ...

(ii.) ...

(iii.) Increased market value of property **of little weight with Land Commissioners** (...)

...

Improvements

Third and Fourth Reports, 1845—continued.

Holland, Mr. H., &c. (Analysis of the Evidence)—continued.

Improvements. Tenant to give particulars of, where claimed and right to such particulars (64-101)......Disregarded by landlord on point of value, but by amount as of little weight compared with tenant-right (65)......Usually claimed by tenant—

  (b.) Drainage.

  (B.) Buildings.

  (31.) Reclamation.

Champerty and value of, noted by Land Commissioners (64-67)......But no judicial opinion given as to weight of such claim (64, 65).

Produce. Reports of, subject of, with Land Commissioners, and laid before Court previous to hearing of appeals (69, 70)......But are often disregarded (71)......Preparations of by valuers (70, 71)......Inspection of (71-77)......Official reports are not cross-examined (71)......Appointments of circuit valuers (78).

Hayes v. Damseth, appeal in case of (106)......Decision in, has had little effect in fixing of rents (107)......Not applicable to rates affected by Ulster Charters (106).

I.

Improvements, class of, usually claimed by tenant (Holmes 60-64).

    (b.) *Buildings, as (Barton 155-158; 161; Chandos 1706, 1867).*

    (B.) *Drainage, as (Rogers 188, 189; Chandos 1700-1711, 1715-1716, 1745-1746; Smith 1446-1452, 2855-2857, 2862-1865; Gray 1956-1962, 1964, 1981, 2011-2044).*

    (31.) *Fences, as (Barton 161-163; Smith 337-345; Wright 1676-1596, 1683, 1686, 1688; Chandos 1760-1764, 1756, 1767).*

    (34.) *Reclamation, as (Recma 170, 171; Chandos 1683-1686, 1766-1769; Gray 2000-2002, 2014-2024)......Great difficulty, in some cases, in proceedings in case of (Gray 2096-2097).*

  (r.) *Manuring, as (Gray 2029).*

Questions as to (Foley 596-600; Baldwin 1388, 1081, 1118; Chandos 1742, 1743).

————————. *Arising under Ulster Custom (Holmes 49).*

Allowances made for, by Sub-Commissioners (Smith 599; Foley 645, 700, 714-717, 828, 815-816, 865-868, 866-872, 884, 885-897).

Erratic in regard, of Sub-Commissioners (Smith 511, 512, 516).

Evidence as to, taken by Sub-Commissioners (Smith 466-494).

Details of, given by Sub-Commissioners (Recma 201-208, 210; Smith 466).

Forms as to, to be filled up by Sub-Commissioners (Lyle p. 839) (Smith 579, 878, 874-868, 898, 808, 816, 822; Baldwin 1091-1095, 1123, 1127).

Character and Value of, noted by Land Commissioners (Holmes 84-87; Recma 708).

Particulars of, required, when claimed by tenant (Holmes 94, 101; Recma 107, 140; Smith 342, 343, 368, 364, 868; Wright 1648, 1614; Chandos 1693-1696).

Notice to Landlord of, when claimed (Smith 343-345, 362, 363; Foley 390-390).

Value of tenants' (Smith 360; Foley 778-713; Smith 1818-1893, 1836-1837, 1848-1849).

Possible claim for, after fifteen years, having been already allowed for (Smith 396, 397; Baldwin 1278-1281; Chandos 1675, 1778).

Compensation for, not tenant-right: tenant unable to claim (Holmes 95; Foley 702).

Supposed as to, extravagant and occasional difficulty of reconciling evidence (Recma 146-153).

Buildings as to, See Fence.

Mode of taking into consideration (Gray 1974-1978).

Recent, of, when dealt with (Baldwin 1083-1090)......Considered as point of issue by landlord, but of little weight compared with tenant-right by tenant (Holmes 86).

L.

Laboure. Cottages of, provision of Act as regards (Recma 333-334) — Often superior to those of tenant (Recma 338).

Land. Letting value of (Recma 800, 806, 398; Foley 670, 745; Baldwin 1008-1010, 1412, 1438).

Market value of (Holmes 110; Recma 388-293; Smith 838-649; Foley 787-749; Baldwin 1050, 1828).

Value

Third and Fourth Reports, 1883—continued.

Land—continued.

Value of, in proportion to taxes (Salaburia 1486, 1447.; **Chambre 1791**).

—— Accumulation of holdings (Chambre 1728, **1793**).

Questions of easier, of, decided by Lay Sub-Commissioner. **See Sub-Commissioner.**

Valuation of. See *Valuation.*

Acquisition of, by Land Commissioners (Madden 188, 245, 244—246, 194—196; Riley 467, 788—791, 378, 331; Baldwin 1175—1188, 1284, 1331—1313; Chambre 1691—1696, 1787—1789; Gray 1924—1927, 1928—1963, 1982, 1983).

—— Preparation made by tenant for (Gray 2008, 2016).

—— By value (Riley 1894—1920, 1924, 1926, 1932, 2043, 2044—2045, 2051, 2059, 2061—2067).

Determination of (Madden 226, 229, 300; Smith 946, 461; Riley 742, 821—841; Baldwin 3031—3053, 1466; Wright 1681, 1692—1621, 1694; Gray 2095—2098, 2082—2084).

Sale of (Riley 629; Baldwin 1503, 1504, 1567)—— Costs in hundred of. **See Landlord.**

Investment in, primary instrument for (Riley 164—190; Smith 662; **Baldwin 1503**, 1536)——Of money in (Baldwin 1425, 1471—1476, 1476—1478).

Purchase of, by tenant. See *Tenant.*

—— in Encumbered Estates Court (Baldwin **1410**).

Right of recovery. See *Riley.*

Sub-division of small holdings (Baldwin 1547—1566, 1584).

Redistribution of (Baldwin 1546—1556, 1563).

Reclamation of. See *Improvements and Reclamation.*

Land Commission (Digital) Court. *Appeals made to.* See *Appeal.*

Formation and constitution of (Baldwin 1218—1220).

Heading of (Wright 1610, 1623—1624).

Judgment of, mode of giving (Baldwin 17).

Decisions of, reliance on which given (Holmes 47, 114; Smith 409—413)——Difference in, regards estimating of rent (Holmes 96).

Improvements, character of, noted by (Holmes 44—57)——But no judicial opinion given as to weight of such questions (Holmes 58, 63).

Rent, reduction of, no indication given to depreciation on which made (Holmes 91).

Decision, Principle of, no decision given as to, as to be decided by Sub-Commissioners (Holmes 111).

Official Valuer &c. See *Valuer.*

Reports of return, value attached to (Holmes 66; Smith 394—397, 998, 991—998; Baldwin 1256—1258, 1561, 1562; Wright 1659—1664, 1688—1691; Smith 1964).

Sale of, as regards cost in, again. See *Appeal.*

Land Commission Court, *duration of, interruption, and ...* (Holmes 8—11)——*Distance of, from certain courts of justice* (Holmes 8, 11)——*Manner of Land Commissioners for not removing from* (Holmes 10)——*Has same Peer Courts* (Holmes 10—14)——*Days of sittings of* (Holmes 17)——*Cases before* (Holmes 4; Smith 826, 834).

Land Law (Ireland) Act, 1881, working of, before county courts (Holmes 1066, 1081).

—— *Working of* (Riley 708; Baldwin 1000—1063, 1242—1263, 1913—1915, 1260, 1261, 1965, 1413—1420, 1486, 1487—1490; Wright 1587—1641; Chambre 1897; O'Connor Don 2065, 2383).

—— *with regard to—*

(i.) *Drainage* (Baldwin 1587—1739; Chambre 1717—1720, 1726).

(ii.) *Restoration* (Holdings 1459, 1464).

(iii.) *Emigration* (Holdings 1469, 1472, 1480).

Purchase Clauses of, working of (Smith 648—652; **Baldwin 1453, 1455—1488, 1491, 1498, 1516, 1621**; O'Connor Don 2387, 2388).

Purchase of Holdings under. See *Purchase.*

Rent, Fixture of, under. See *Rent.*

Administration of, cost of (Baldwin 1374—1380, 1394—1397, 1424—1438).

Labourers' Dwellings, provision of, as regards. See *Labourer.*

Landlord, lessee to, under. See *Landlord.*

(138—141.)   E 3   **Landlord**

Third and Fourth Reports, 1883—continued.

Inspection

Third and Fourth Reports, 1882—continued.

—— —— is

Third and Fourth Reports, 1883—*continued*.

Rent, Fixture of—continued.

——— in cases of sheep runs (*Baldwin* 1295–1306, 1362, 1364, 1398–1403).

——— on reclaimed ground (*Chamber* 1663–1666).

——— on investment land (*Chamber* 1667–1690).

——— when middlemen interested (*Reeves* 316–334; *Smith* 627–639; *Foley* 878–882).

Reductions of (*Holmes* 21–23, 32, 36; *Reeves* 258–263, 285, 286, 303; *Smith* 371, 373, 387–432, 433, 439, 430, 627–636; *Foley* 699, 700, 712–715, 822–834, 844–952, 957–960, 992–994; *Baldwin* 1238–1259, 1262–1276, 1343–1347, 1360–1366, 1382, 1396, 1408; *Wright* 1584–1612, 1613; *Chamber* 1644, 1647)——Average of (*Baldwin* 1245–1345; *Gray* 1930, 1931; *O'Conor Don* 2161).

Small reductions of, made by Land Commissioners (*Smith* 460, 490; *Foley* 948–950; *Wright* 1613, 1625, 1638; *Gray* 1930).

Payment of, by tenant (*Holmes* 111; *Reeves* 172, 173, 179, 184–189, 204, 210).

Original rent, left unaltered (*Foley* 767–771)——Raised (*Holmes* 36; *Foley* 769–772).

Judicial, date from which, held due (*Smith* 1548–1554).

Report, from official valuers. *See Valuers*.

Of proceedings of Sub-Commissioners (*Foley* 783–784; *Smith* 1833).

Rundale System. Arrangement of property under (*Baldwin* 1339–1341)——Maps necessary in cases of (*Baldwin* 1109–1113, 1115–1119).

S.

Sheep Runs. Fixture of rent in cases of (*Baldwin* 1295–1306, 1362, 1364, 1398–1403)——Difference in decisions, as regards (*Baldwin* 1307–1310)——Usually advantageous to tenant (*Baldwin* 1398).

Smith, Mr. G. H. (Analysis of his Evidence.)—Has practised before Courts of Land Commission (339, 340)——Also under Land Act, 1870 (340–342).

Appeal Court. Principle on which cases before, decided (409–414)——Depend on reports of Court valuers in questions of value, no evidence as to value being given before Court (584–587)——That reports of valuers not always acted upon (588–603).

Appeals to, seldom made (609, 610, 620).

——— *Costs* in, rules as to (617–619).

——— Difficulty of making (624, 625).

——— Disinclination of Land Commissioners to allow (624, 630).

——— Rules of Land Commissioners as to (548–555, 660–670).

Decisions of Land Commissioners. Reasons for often applied for (482, 498)——Many cases settled out of Court owing to uncertainty of decisions, though such settlements neither legal nor binding (497, 502).

Of Sub-Commissioners, usually confirmed on appeal (419, 416–523)——Apparently given in favour of tenant (389).

Land Act. Provision of buildings under, not likely to occur (648–651)——Amount of money borrowed under, for purposes of buildings unlikely to be paid (652).

Sub-Commission. Reports of proceedings before (1833)——Virtually under control of Lay Sub-Commissioners (483–487).

Sub-Commissioners, Procedure of, rapid (395, 396)——Possibility of being deceived as to drainage (1845).

Legal Sub-Commissioner, legal questions to be decided by (485, 489).

Removal of (Mr. Fitzgerald). Reason for (422–424)——Difference of decisions after his removal (425–427).

Mr. Mack, Sub-Commission under. Greater reductions of rent made by, although on same class of land (363, 383, 417–433)——Such rents having been paid for number of years (436)——Such decisions confirmed on appeal (428–436).

Form ("Tenant-right which includes all improvements"), used only by Sub-Commission under Mr. Mack (372, 374, 654, 383)——All forms filled up by that Sub-Commission signed by Mr. Mack (375)——Although neither legal member of Sub-Commission (376)——Nor having any legal knowledge (383, 384)——Reasons for forms being thus signed (377, 378)——In all other cases particulars of improvements given, and forms signed by legal Sub-Commissioner (378, 379, 380)——No observation made by Land Commissioners on forms being signed by Mr. Mack (381, 382)——Speech made by Mr. Mack (384–391).

Third and Fourth Reports, 1881—continued.

Third and Fourth Reports, 1881—continued.

Sub-Commission, Composition of, Result of (Reeve 292, 301-306)—Changes in composition of (Holmes 20, 31, 32; Reeve 737-738)—Such alterations conducive to better valuation of rents (Hobbs 28, 30).

Arrangement of (Holmes 288; Foley 768-800, 851, 855, 862-864; Baldwin 1172, 1173, 1314, 1315).

Proceedings of, Records of (Foley 768-784; Smith 1633)—Virtually under control of lay members (Smith 461-467).

Evidence given before, weight of (Wright 1344-1349, 1356).

Decisions, differences of (Hudson 33, 34; Robinson 1633).

——— in different members of same Sub-Commission (Holmes 42-46, 48, 44; Reeve 839-845, 849)—Affected by changes in composition of Sub-Commission (Reeve 735).

Procedure of (Reeve 136, 137, 145; Chamier 1162-1620; Gray 1981, 1982).

Rent-increasing tendency to reduce (Nelson 114-128).

Sub-Commissioner, Pensions of, Method of (Baldwin 1014, 1017, 1040, 1069-1072, 1616).

Popularity of (Baldwin 1437, 1441, 1442).

Tenure of Office, by (Foley 558; Baldwin 1008, 1008, 1322; Gray 1920-1993).

Removal of, reasons for (Holmes 139, 131; Nelson 412, 424; Foley 669-671; Chamier 1748, 1749).

Changes of (Holmes 21; Foley 647, 651; Baldwin 1149, 1158-1160; Chamier 1155).

——— result of (Holmes 23, 24, 42, 111; Smith 407-429, 431; Baldwin 1149, 1151, 1145-1158; Chamier 1741-1745, 1749).

Procedure of (Holmes 110; Reeve 141, 145; Smith 368, 490; Foley 595, 595, 658, 677-681; Gray 1955-1957).

——— No instructions as to, given (Reeve 160, 236, 239, 311-314; Foley 737, 739).

——— with regard to tenant-right (Smith 400).

——— ——— ——— figures on improvements (Smith 437-441).

Registration, alterations made by, for. See Improvement.

Tenant-right, Allowance made for. See Ulster Custom.

Rent, Fixing of. See Rent.

Revision of, Attempts to. See Revision.

——— principle of. See Revision.

——— continued on appeal (Hobbs 116; Smith 433-436, 517, 520; Foley 590, 591; Wright 1344-1349).

——— reversed on appeal (Reeve 330).

——— Reasons for, not given to Land Commissioners (Reeve 219-226, 221, 226).

——— Questions not to reopen for. See Revision.

——— Reason of, greater than others afford value attached to Sub-Commission (Reeve 253, 257).

——— Record of grounds for, no official kept (Reeve 223-226)—Nor of particulars of claim made (Chamier 1671-1674, 1877).

——— Of Chief Commissioners, as to date from which judicial rents date, not followed by (Smith 1848-2854).

Produce, Price of, considered by. See Produce.

Tenant, Benefit received by, from holding, considered by. See Tenant.

Land, Condition market value of, and depreciation of. See Land.

Rent, Consider fair rent to be paid. See Rent.

——— Small reductions of, make. See Rent.

Inspection of Holdings, by. See Land.

Valuation of Holdings, by. See Valuation.

——— Instructions given, as to (Smith 473, 476).

Maps, necessary to. See Maps.

Improvements, present value of, not given by (Smith 460; Foley 689-791).

——— Allowances made for. See Improvements.

——— Possibility of fixing doubted as to (Smith 1448).

——— Particulars of claimed, order for, to county (Smith 343, 347, 354, 360).

Third and Fourth Reports, 1888—continued.

Third and Fourth Reports, 1883—continued.

Third and Fourth Reports, 1882—continued.

Valuers, &c.—continued.

Reports given to Appeal Court. See *Land Commission Appeal Court.*
— Sub-Commissioners, dependent on (*Baldwin* 1130).
— released in, by Land Commissioners (*Nichols* 46; *Rams* 233).
— Inspector of (*Holmes* 72–73; *Smith* 802).
— structure of table (*Nichols* 1127–1128, 1836; 1892–1894; *Wright* 1639).
— decision of Sub-Commissioners with regard to (*Smith* 479).
— Rules laid in (*Foley* 555–556, 558, 566).
Evidence in Chief, not bound by (*Gray* 1567, 1584–1586).
Sub-Commissioners, assistance given to, by valuers (*Moran* 514; 518).
— — duties of, as regards (*Reeves* 233; *Smith* 479).
Decrease of, value of (Nichols 69, 68, 72, 73; Davies 188; Smith 582–587, 592, 894–898; Robson 1041, 1298–1283, 1321, 1322; Chandler 1646, 1651, 2196–1919, 1973–1816).
Farm to be filled up, by (App. p. 80) (Gray 1959, 1973).
Revision of (Rules 256–259; 1884–1894, 1900–1905).
Valuation of. See Valuation.
Evidence of Report, not upheld by (Smith 1827).
Evidence of, acting for landlord (Foley 574).
— — — — — tenant (Foley 575, 887–889).
Voter Clauses, interest of tenant under, regarded by (Holmes 62–155).
Map of Holding, necessary to (*Baldwin* 1157, 1158, 1164, 1174).

W.

Wright, Mr. C., Barrister-at-Law. (Analysis **of his Evidence.**)

Land Commission (Appeal) Court, unsatisfactory working of (1519, 1525–1531).
Dependent on valuations of official valuers (1595–1600).— Although such valuations not always acted on (1629–1631).
Employers of Land Commissioners, Inspector of (1594–1596, 1572–1574, 1598–1608, 1610).—As increases given in (1584–1587, 1590, 1595–1600, 1637).
Sub-Commissioners, Decisions of, abolition in character of (1538).
— — — — — seldom altered on appeal (1564–1565).
Evidence, given before (1544–1548, 1550).
Land, Deterioration of, allowed for by Sub-Commissioners (1581, 1592–1594, 1594).
Buildings on, Evaluation of, by Sub-Commissioners (1589–1590).
Rent, Fixture of, by Land Commissioners (1547–1553, 1573, 1587–1594, 1601, 1602, 1604, 1616–1620, 1623, 1625).
Reduction of, although having been paid for number of years (1614–1615).—When buildings purchased within short time (1615).—Small alterations of, made by Sub-Commissioners (1623, 1625, 1626).
Land Act, 1881, experience in working of (1537–1541).
Profits, value of, not considered by Sub-Commissioners (1609–1612).
Improvements, Evaluation of, difficulty arising from, and being given by tenant (1584).
— — — — — claimed by tenant (1614).
— — **—** Increase, considered as (1574–1580, 1583, 1586, 1588).
Gate, no information as to history of, given to official valuers (1623).